THE IRON MEN OF VENUS

By
DON WILCOX

I0541532

ARMCHAIR FICTION & MUSIC
PO Box 4369, Medford, Oregon 97504

*For more information about Armchair Books and products, visit our
website at…*

www.armchairfiction.com

Or email us at…

armchairfiction@yahoo.com

METAL MONSTROSITIES FROM ANOTHER WORLD

They came up out of the sea to strike terror into the hearts of men—giant lumbering robots that sent panic-stricken citizens scurrying in all directions. Even worse, they seemed almost unstoppable, and before long it was clear they were out to destroy everything and everyone in their path. At first no one had the slightest clue as to their origin, but soon the inevitable speculation arose—were these towering monsters from Earth, or were they the invasion forerunners from another planet?

Don Wilcox was one of the most prolific authors of the golden age of pulp science fiction. His fiction is a pure joy to read. His novels and stories were a mainstay in renowned magazines like "Amazing Stories" and "Fantastic Adventures." Here is one of his last published novels.

FOR A SECOND COMPLETE NOVEL, TURN TO PAGE 83

CAST OF CHARACTERS

JOE KANE

He was a mechanic, just your average Joe, but he found himself accused of complicity in an interplanetary conspiracy.

PAUL MADDERGALL

A big-shot investigator in way over his head...he was determined to find a scapegoat, but did he himself have something to hide?

DYNAMO

He worked at a steel plant where the last batch of metal received gave him the creeps—literally.

COMMANDER DOYLE

A tough veteran space commander. He didn't want to hear supposition—he wanted action.

RUPPERT KANE

He had a reputation as a planet-trotting playboy and was wanted for murder—but was he really all that bad?

ZUBER

His scheme for power was going along just as he'd planned—so what was making him so uneasy?

CHAPTER ONE

THEY HAD placed the red knife on the table and Joe Kane saw it there when he took the witness chair. It stood pointing straight up like a candlestick, resting on the squared-off end of the white handle. The blade glistened red, not blood red but the deep metallic red of Venus steel. Joe's lips went dry as the men fired questions at him.

"Your name? Address? Age? Occupation?"

Joe was twenty-seven. He lived in one of the low-priced underground apartment houses. He was a troubleshooter on an interplanetary freight line.

"Now, Mr. Kane, do you recognize this knife?"

"That particular knife? No."

"You've never seen such a knife before?"

"I've seen such knives—yes. Everyone has. Pictures of them, anyway. Anyone that reads the newspapers—"

"What does the knife mean to you, Mr. Kane?"

"It's a Venus knife. It's made of Venus steel." Joe wondered what all this had to do with him. He wished they would get on with it. Staying away from work was costing him eight dollars an hour.

"Go on, Mr. Kane. Tell us what this particular Venus knife means."

Joe's gray eyes narrowed. He knew the face of this important man barking the questions. This was Paul Maddergall, the big-shot investigator who often made the headlines. His face reminded Joe of an arrowhead, blunt of features and hard as flint. He wore a fresh red bow tie, and Joe thought the red of the Venus knife reflected in his glittering dark eyes.

"You're stalling, Mr. Kane. What is the meaning of this knife? Isn't it a symbol of some kind?"

"It's a sign of danger. They say it's a threat of death."
Joe's brain was in a whirl. How did these questions concern
him?

"A threat from whom?"

THE IRON MEN
OF VENUS

BY DON WILCOX

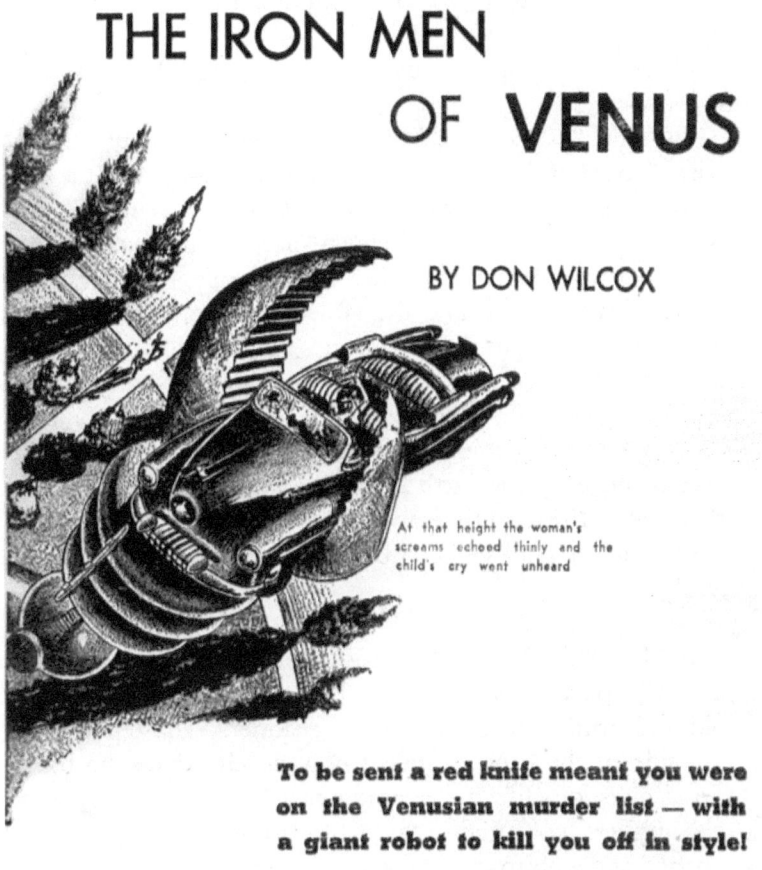

At that height the woman's screams echoed thinly and the child's cry went unheard

To be sent a red knife meant you were on the Venusian murder list — with a giant robot to kill you off in style!

"From the killers that live on the Storm Continent of Venus. It's the special trade mark of the criminal colony."

"Did you call them killers, Mr. Kane?"

"That's what they call them in the newspapers."

Maddergall gave a sly smile. The other men around the table shuffled restlessly, but Maddergall would not be hurried. "Killers is a very strong term, Mr. Kane. We do carry on commerce with them, don't we?"

"Yes, sir."

"We recognize them as an interplanetary colony, don't we?"

"Yes, sir. I understand they were originally a criminal colony."

"Originally—yes. A few generations ago—but let that pass. The point is, you have called them killers. That makes them sound like savages or wild animals. Isn't it true, Mr. Kane, that they are human beings—like you and me?"

"They're not like me," Joe said sharply. He saw that some of the men around the table were suppressing smiles. The chairman called for order. Anger showed in Paul Maddergall's stony face.

"Meaning what?" Maddergall barked.

"They're bloodthirsty and dangerous, and they'd like to take revenge on the earth by sticking knives in our backs— that's what I read in the papers." Joe did his best to hold his voice calm. "They've been bumping off our ships right and left."

PAUL MADDERGALL rose from his chair heavily and began to pace. For a man in his mid-thirties, he was old— old and brittle and cutting in his manner. The reporters at the side of the room watched him closely. Now he began firing questions like a machine gun. Joe's face grew warm, his answers confused. Suddenly, to his relief, the door opened and a uniformed porter called in.

"Pardon me, gentlemen, but is Mr. Joe Kane in here? I have a message for Joe Kane."

The chairman started to order the porter out. "No interruptions, please. Mr., Kane is busy. Sergeant-at-arms, please remove—"

But Joe had risen instantly. The porter was ushered out, the door was closed, and again the room came to order.

"We were speaking of the red knife," Maddergall resumed, gesturing toward Exhibit A in the center of the table. "Mr. Kane, if you discovered such a knife on your desk, point up—as the late Senator Droondair did—what would you conclude?"

"That someone from the Venus Storm Continent had put it there—"

"And—"

"And that he intended to murder me."

"Now we're getting somewhere. By the way, what did happen to Senator Droondair?"

"He was murdered."

"Why, Mr. Kane? What was back of that cruel assassination?"

Joe touched his perspiring temples. "Well, I read an article about the case—"

"Speak up, Joe Kane. Why do you think Senator Droondair was murdered?"

"I suppose it was on account of the Droondair Bill. He wanted a law to abolish trade with the colony."

THE CHAIRMAN, John Helva, a large, black-haired man with frosted eyebrows, rose and tapped the table with the gavel. Time was short, he said. The questioners must bear in mind that Joe Kane was not being tried for the murder of Senator Droondair or anyone else. "There are no charges against Joe Kane, gentlemen. We're looking for his older brother, Ruppert Kane. Joe may be able to help us locate him: Please confine your questions—"

So it was Ruppert they wanted. Joe's worries shifted gears. Whatever these men were trying to get at, Joe's instant determination to protect his brother was full of complications. Ruppert, a playboy planet-trotter, had hob-nobbed with the Venus killers as though they were fraternity brothers.

"You have two brothers? Correct?"

"Correct."

"The youngest is a pilot on a Mars line?"

"Yes, sir. That's Lanny. He's a good pilot."

"And Ruppert, the oldest—" Here Maddergall began sniping in earnest. He asked a dozen questions about Ruppert's space travels, never waiting for an answer. When he paused, Joe admitted in bewilderment, "That's Ruppert, all right. He does get around."

"He is known to have visited the penal colony on Venus?"

"Yes."

"Several times?"

"Yes."

"He must have friends in that colony."

"That's possible. He's interested in all kinds of people, good and bad."

"Even the so-called killers?"

Joe hesitated. "I guess he figures they're human beings, like you and me."

Again the smiles around the table broke in upon Maddergall's severity. His flinty eyes went ablaze with a dangerous fury. "Mr. Kane, your impertinence impresses no one. You will confine your answers to yes or no. Did your brother Ruppert ever possess a knife like this?"

"Not to my knowledge."

"Did he ever lend it to you?"

Joe's teeth tightened. "I said that he never, to my knowledge—"

"Answer yes or no. Did he ever lend his knife to you?"

"No."

"Then you admit he possessed such a knife?"

"No, I did not admit—"

"And he refused to lend it to you."

Joe leaned forward his fists clenched. "He did not refuse to lend it. I said—"

"Oh, then he did lend it to you? That's what we wanted to know."

"He did not. How could he, when he didn't even—"

"Mr. Kane, you're confusing your story like a school boy who has ditched. Now think, and answer me yes or no. Did your brother Ruppert ever lend you his Venus knife?"

"No."

Maddergall turned to the others with a concluding gesture. "There, the investigating committee will please note that Joe Kane has admitted, under oath, that his brother Ruppert, a friend of the Venus killers, did possess a Venus knife of the sort used for death threats—perhaps the same knife used to threaten the late Senator Droondair."

Joe's brain spun. He saw the news reporters jump for the telephones, and he could imagine the black headlines. Guilt flooded through him. Somehow, in his confusion, he had let Ruppert down. But it was all a mistake. He hadn't said those things. He hadn't—

He blurted, "It's a lie. I didn't say it. You can't print those things." He sprang from his chair and tried to make a path for Maddergall. "I won't stand for this. My brother is innocent. If they print what you said, I'll—"

He came at Maddergall, not sure what he was doing or saying. The men seized him, caught his arms, and held him back. At the same time Paul Maddergall grabbed the knife. At the sight of Maddergall's action, Joe stopped cold. He yelled out, and his tone was a hiss of accusation.

"Look at that. This man grabs a Venus knife…look at him. He's threatening me…giving me the death threat."

The sergeant-at-arms slapped a hand over Joe's mouth and flung him back to his seat. Joe bounced up, holding out his open hands to show he hadn't intended to fight—he only wanted them to see Maddergall and the knife. But he didn't get a chance to say what was in his mind. The sergeant-at-arms plunged at him again with a swinging fist that might have been a baseball bat as far as Joe was concerned. The blow caught him on the jaw and knocked him sprawling across the floor.

CHAPTER TWO

HE LIMPED down the steps, paused to take a deep breath, and turned to look back at the building from which he had emerged. It was adorned with some slogans about justice, but he wasn't in the mood to read. He looked down at the line of taxis and spotted one with a round, harmless-looking young fellow in the back seat. It was good to know that Dan Dinkins, his buddy, was waiting for him.

Dinkins, known by his friends as "Dynamo", opened the door for him and ordered the taxi driver to cruise down the avenue. "Just as well take the morning off, Joe. It's half shot already, and you look like you are too. What's the matter? Kinda rugged?"

Joe mopped his face and rubbed his jaw. "We'll take the whole day off." He loosened his collar. He was perspiring like a Turkish bath. How his pal Dynamo could wear a topcoat on a summer day was more than he could fathom—but that was Dynamo. He wouldn't be Dynamo without that battered old gabardine with its many inside pockets, stuffed with everything imaginable; it made him look like an overstuffed tent on feet. Just now he drew a bottle of grape pop, mysteriously chilled, from one of his inner compartments. He opened it and handed it to Joe.

"You look like you could use a sip of your favorite brew...don't mention it...so it was rough, huh?"

"Like a washboard. They drubbed me on both sides."

"What's their angle?"

Joe let the purple juice gurgle down his throat, and the taxi driver glanced back enviously. Joe said, "They're trying to get something on Ruppert."

Dynamo's grin gave way to a dill pickle look and he groaned.

"I know you've got no use for Ruppert," Joe said. "Lots

of folks don't understand Ruppert. But he's my brother, and I'm not going to see them hang a murder on him when some Venus Killer is the guilty party. Ruppert never had anything against Senator Droondair."

"Oh, that." Dynamo pretended to flick a bit of dust from his coat. "They should know they'd never get you to say anything against Ruppert. Though what he's ever done for you or Lanny is more than I can figure."

"We've had our differences," Joe admitted, "but after all, he is my brother. I can't understand all his fool notions, travelling out to rub elbows with those Venus devils. But Lanny and I have learned to take him as he is." Joe changed the subject abruptly. "Where are we driving, and why."

"Just giving you a chance to cool off. You're sweating like a bowl of cannibal soup."

"Might as well drive back to our apartment. There might be some mail—which reminds me—" Joe started to reach for something he remembered putting in his inside coat pocket.

"It reminds me, too," said Dynamo. "Who's pulling the gags with the Venus knives?"

"Huh?" Joe saw that Dynamo was fishing into the depths of that big mystery-packed coat again.

"I just came from our apartment before I picked you up. I figured to bring you your mail, if any—which there wasn't. But I saw this." He brought forth a shining ten-inch knife with a red steel blade and a white handle.

Joe glared. "Not another one of those."

Dynamo's grin faded. "So it ain't just a gag you're pulling on Lanny?"

"Gag, he says." Joe felt himself grow pale. "Where did you find it?"

"On Lanny's desk—over there in the living room. Sticking up like a lightning rod. It didn't blend in right with the furniture, so I picked it up."

"Well, I'll be." Joe placed the fingertips of both hands on

his forehead and brushed them slowly down over his cheeks. Then he locked his hands together behind his head and fairly passed out into the realm of his own thoughts.

The taxi driver glanced back, Dynamo said, "Keep driving."

PRESENTLY Joe grumbled, "I'm in the mood for a fight."

"You don't have to tell me. I know the symptoms."

"I'm not talking about a schoolboy fight with the lads on the freight crew. I mean a real fight."

"Okay, okay. We'll mop up on the Venus killers, just you and me," Dynamo responded with a straight face. He lifted a sarcastic eyebrow.

"It's about time, when they start sneaking in your homes, leaving a knife one day and slitting your throat the next." Joe took the knife, weighed it in his hand, and passed it back to Dynamo. "I'd sure hate to think anyone is gunning for Lanny. Ruppert and I raised him."

"Least of all would you suspect Ruppert, of course." Dynamo buried the knife somewhere within his coat. His last remark could have been left unsaid as far as Joe was concerned. They rode along in strained silence until Dynamo changed the key. "I agree with you, Joe, those killers are seeping in, one way and another. I'm getting darned suspicious of the trade we carry on with them."

"How do you mean?"

"The steel they're shipping to my boss, Old Man Zuber, has got the creeps. I've been meaning to tell you. Why don't we drive out that way as long as we're killing the day?" Dynamo called an order to the taxi driver and they spun off the avenue and out along the wide highway toward the Zuber Oceanside Industries.

The driver took advantage of a red light and bought a noon paper, promptly losing himself in the headlines. The light changed, and Dynamo said, "Push 'er along, friend.

You'll have plenty of time to do your reading later."

THEY DROVE as far around the grounds as a side road would take them. They told the driver to wait there; they would be back in half an hour. They struck out and walked along the fence toward the cliff above the deep Atlantic. The sun blazed down. Joe removed his coat, but not Dynamo.

Hiking along past the no-trespassing signs, Joe got a close-up view of the great beams of metal that the Zuber plant was shipping in from Venus. Slices of green and red metals, two and three hundred feet long, lay in rows, gleaming in the noon sun.

"The irony of it," Joe said. "What a trick of fate." He was thinking of the penal colony that the earth governments had once established on the Storm Continent of Venus. In that wasteland the convicts had discovered unlimited quantities of the finest metals known to man.

"They've got all they want up there," Dynamo said, "and the devil of it is, they know how to use it. Even the scrap that they toss off to Old Man Zuber has got a lot of tricks in it."

"I'm still in the dark."

"That's what I brought you out to see," Dynamo said, leading the way along the fence. "Keep an eye open. Some of these big pieces we've shipped in recently don't stay put. I've been on guard nights and I swear I've seen them move along like big iron snails. Watch close down this way, and you'll—" Then in a quick warning whisper, "Drop. Here comes someone. We shouldn't be seen here."

The fence around the Zuber acres extended down a slope where a quarter of a mile of cliff had worn away. Two men were approaching along a path within the fence, slowing their pace as they plodded up the grade. Back of the rocks and bushes on the seaward side of the fence Joe and Dynamo hid themselves and waited. Dynamo whispered, "Of all the devils...if it ain't the big boss himself."

"Zuber?"

"Yeah, the fat one in the white suit. The scrawny one they call Mouse. He's a big executive in the boss's office. Quiet little guy, but nobody crosses him. They say he's a brain."

"Listen. " Joe whispered.

The talking became audible. Zuber was puffing and perspiring, but it was plain from his big, gleaming blue eyes that he was as happy as any miser over his store of metal wealth.

"Yes, I quite agree with what you say," Mouse spoke in a tin-like voice. "But let me ask you, Zuber, have you noticed anything peculiar about these bars we've been getting lately?"

"Peculiar?"

"Very peculiar," the thin voice said.

"It's all scrap, Moberly. We're buying it all at scrap prices—with the aid of government subsidies, thanks to Maddergall. Rich deal, Moberly. What more could we ask?"

"Some of this metal is alive, Zuber. Believe me."

"Alive? What are you saying?"

"It's got live stuff in it. Anyway it moves."

"Concealed motors, perhaps? Those Venus boys are much farther along than anyone would guess. All right, we'll bust the stuff apart when the time comes, and pull out any internal power units they've left in. The main thing is to get more of it—more and more and more!"

"That's one of your three major plans, I understand," said Mouse Moberly, helping the big man up over a difficult step. They paused within ten feet of Joe and Dynamo's hiding place.

"And the other two are, keep the Venus killers eating out of our hands, and promise them a chance to come back under our arrangement."

"Of course. *Our*—that is, *your*—for you'll be the one great man when that day comes."

"Not necessarily," Zuber said, giving his little companion

a modest smile. "There'll be greatness enough for all of us. You'll be near the top. Maddergall, too. He's moving things in the right direction as fast as possible. Right in the groove, Maddergall is the same as you and me. The main thing is, the plan has got to be so attractive for the killers that they'll fall in, in good order."

"You mean, *after*—"

"*After* they've had their revenge. We can't deny them that. That's what they live for."

The smaller man gazed out at the ocean as if seeing visions. "Yes, Zuber, the bigness of it almost bowls me over. And yet—"

"It's not impossible. We're getting the substance of the whole revolution right here—here in this vast store of Venus metals, and that's why I say to you—"

Zuber broke off sharply. He gave such a quick movement of his arms that Joe wondered if he had suddenly discovered he was being spied upon. But no, he was looking the other way. With a trembling hand he pointed.

"Yes, I saw it," Mouse Moberly said in a low, excited voice. "It moved, didn't it? That's what I was telling you. Look..."

JOE STRETCHED his neck to see a twenty-five foot jointed beam of greenish-silver metal slipping gradually down the long embankment. A small cloud of dust rose around it, and a low dragging noise sounded. It moved down toward a square-shaped piece of similar metal to which other long beams were joined.

Clunk! The end of the sliding beam struck the wider piece with a concussion that made the ground tremble. The piece appeared to lock together, like a giant finger joining onto a hand. Dynamo must have thought of such a similarity, for he whispered to Joe, "Looks to me like a big hand with three fingers and a thumb."

"It fastened on, didn't it?"

"Just like train cars coupling together. It sure as heck belongs there." Then they ducked back and held their silence, for they could hear Zuber and Mouse Moberly talking it over.

"Just a coincidence, you think?" Mouse asked in a thin voice that expressed disbelief.

"Looks to me like the earth slipped a little with the weight," Zuber muttered. "Strange, though, the way it happened to fit up to that big hunk of a hand. A hand, that's what it looks like. Do you see it, Moberly? Those pieces must have belonged together. A part of a big statue, I'd say." He gave a dry laugh and slapped the little man on the back. "Don't lose any sleep over it, boy. Just a coincidence. However, you might get a crew out here sometime in the next week or two and see if there are any power units inside those pieces."

They moved on along the ridge out of hearing of Joe and Dynamo.

"Now you've seen," Dynamo whispered.

"Seen and heard." said Joe.

"You heard what he said about Maddergall and the plot?"

"Did I? Dynamo, they're scheming to bust the whole interplanetary system wide open." Joe was staring with such intensity that he could hardly move until Dynamo tugged at his arm. He was fairly frozen. "Dynamo, we've heard it, both of us, and that means we've got it right on our shoulders."

"We better report to someone."

"To the right persons, nobody else. As quick as we can. What we know is as big as a million atom bombs. If we tell it to the wrong party, it's just plain good-night, world."

"Who'll we tell it to?"

"Only someone we can trust, for sure."

"Someone like your brother? Lanny, I mean. Not Ruppert."

They hurried along and got into the waiting taxi. "We'll

tell Lanny, and the three of us can talk it over. Lanny's due in at noon today from his Mars run. He should be at the space port now."

The taxi spun off toward the highway. Joe, in his excitement, might have been talking louder than necessary, for Dynamo's big elbow gave him a meaningful nudge. The driver glanced around and said, "You got a brother named Lanny?"

"Just keep driving," Joe said. In a lower voice he went on to Dynamo, "Maybe we can get an appointment with Commander Doyle. He's more alert to sky dangers than any other official. He'll listen to us."

The driver glanced around again. "You say you want to go to the space port? "

"That's what we said."

"Your brother happen to be named Lanny Kane?"

"Yes. What about it?"

"You ain't gonna find him at the space port," the driver said.

"How do you mow?"

"They got his picture here in the noon paper. He got killed this morning. He was bringing in a ship. It was two hours out when it blew up. Someone named Lanny Kane was the pilot. I reckon they never knew what hit 'em. So that was your brother?" The driver passed the paper back to them.

Joe stared at it and answered numbly, "That was Lanny, my favorite brother."

CHAPTER THREE

YOU LIKED to see Commander Doyle's face on the television screen. He was a tall, raw-boned man with a high forehead and very direct eyes, very honest, looking right at you as he talked.

"The earth must be better prepared...enemies from

another planet have increased their sniping attacks. We must be ready for trouble."

All around the earth people were listening, on every continent and on the high seas. Out beyond the surface of the earth, too, there were television audiences. Sky stations for interplanetary travelers caught such messages and relayed them. Nearer the earth, fashionable entertainment clubs, hung in space, held up their own programs while the patrons gathered around huge television screens. Little Penny Maddergall, age six, drew closer to her mother as they watched and listened.

"Will we get shot on the way back to the earth, Mamma?" she asked plaintively.

"No, dear, no. You mustn't worry. Listen to what he's saying," her mother whispered. The commander continued:

"...Every Citizen must be ready to do his part. Women and children who live in surface homes should arrange to move in with relatives or friends in underground homes. This it urgent. Do not put it off..."

"Mamma, does that mean they won't kill us if we move underground?"

Claire Maddergall slipped an arm around her child. "You mustn't worry, dear. Daddy and Mamma will look out for you."

"But what about all the other little children?"

"S-s-sh. I'll talk with you later, Penny. Listen to what he's saying."

Little Penny looked around to see her father, Paul Maddergall, coming through the crowd. There were more than three hundred people gathered around the screen at one end of the enclosed deck. This was the "Lazy Meteor," a well known "sky-hung" recreation club, where many government and military personages spent their free time. It was located within two and a half hours of the earth's surface.

Paul Maddergall's face showed a worry as he rejoined his

little family. The day's events had weighed heavily. Worst of all, every television listener around him was scared stiff over another space-ship disaster. The fools looked to him to be able to stop such catastrophes. Little did they know.

Glancing at Claire, her dark eyes shining and her face radiant under the colored lights, he told himself that she was a very glamorous woman. The thought struck him afresh because of something that had occurred earlier in the day—that round he had had with Joe Kane. Only it wasn't Joe he was thinking of; it was Ruppert. Only a few years ago Ruppert Kane had been in love with Claire—maybe still was, who knew? Maddergall smiled to himself. He had been clever enough to win her away from Ruppert Kane, and that was all that mattered.

A sudden dread filled Maddergall as the television programs switched and the day's news came on.

"Look, Daddy, that's you," Penny whispered proudly.

It was a scene from the morning's investigations, and Paul Maddergall stood stiffly as he watched himself and heard his own crisp voice firing the questions.

"Nice going, Paul," someone in the crowd said to him. Other friends glanced about and nodded, as if pleased to find themselves in the presence of so important a man.

But Maddergall's wife only watched in silence.

"Don't take it too seriously, dear," Maddergall whispered to her. "I had to prod him a bit."

"Paul, you're accusing his brother Ruppert of being one of the Venus killers."

"Nothing of the kind, dear."

"That's going too far, Paul. You know Ruppert Kane wouldn't—" Claire Maddergall broke off, biting her lip.

"Hmm. So you're still carrying the torch for that no-good bum. I had often wondered. Now I know." Maddergall froze into stony silence, watching her out of the corner of his eye. She pretended not to hear him, keeping her eyes glued on the television screen. The scene moved abruptly, to

Maddergall's relief, without showing him grab the knife from the table. But the commentator spoke of a bit of roughhouse, in which the fresh young witness learned a thing or two.

"Look, they're fighting," Penny cried. "Daddy, did he try to hurt you?"

On the screen Joe Kane could be seen rising from his chair, holding out his open hands, trying to say something, and the sergeant-at-arms was shown slugging him. Next he was shown picking himself up off the floor.

"But Daddy, why did the man hit him?"

Penny's questions were abruptly hushed by both her parents. A few jovial spirits from the crowd turned to joke with Paul Maddergall over the brisk skirmish. "You meet all kinds of characters in your business, eh, Maddergall? Better carry a gun. Or do you?" But Claire Maddergall only asked to be excused, and she and little Penny wandered away to another part of the deck...

KANE and Dinkins sat in their underground apartment in deep gloom. Dynamo watched the television news through the scene of Joe's being mauled, and muttered, "So that's how you got your swollen face." Joe said nothing. The news went on, giving flashes from the memorial service he and Dynamo had attended late in the afternoon for Lanny Kane and the others who had been lost in the spaceship explosion.

"They're getting it down to routine," Dynamo said. "Disaster in the morning, service in the afternoon, newscast at night; maybe the same thing again tomorrow."

"He was a swell kid," Joe said quietly. "We're going to miss him around here. Who do you suppose planted that knife? They must have known what was coming."

"Sure. Sure they knew." Dynamo glanced at his watch. "Time for me to get over to the plant. I've got a night of work to do."

"Thanks for sticking with me all day, Dynamo." Joe drew a deep breath. "Maybe I'll ride over with you."

"Come along. The air will do you good."

"Yeah. Besides, I remember something I left over that way this morning. I put my coat down when we were eavesdropping on Zuber."

"You'll have a heck of a time finding it out there in the dark. Better steer clear of the guards."

"I'm in the mood to prowl," Joe said in an aggressive voice.

"Well, don't take any chances. After all, what's a coat?"

"It had a letter in it."

"Something important?"

"I never got to open it. Things have been happening so fast." Joe led the way out the door.

"Did you ever get in touch with Commander Doyle?"

"They tried three times and he was always busy. They think I can see him tomorrow, but maybe I'll try again later tonight. This business of losing Lanny has sort of knocked the props out from under me. Before that happened I was ready to go find Paul Maddergall and whip him. If I thought he had anything to do with Lanny's raw deal—"

"Sure he has. It's all one big net." Dynamo hailed a taxi and they rode off down the lighted streets toward the darkness beyond the city. He shuffled among his overloaded pockets. "Anything you need for your prowl? Flashlight? Rope? I've got a compass if you think you'll get lost. Care for a pair of water wings? The ocean's deep off that cliff."

"Thanks anyway." Joe managed to chuckle a good night as he dropped off.

THAT NIGHT air was exhilarating. Troubles were heavy, but Joe was beginning to see his own clear purpose through it all. He talked to himself with quiet determination as he trudged along the fence where he and Dynamo had walked earlier in the day. It was one thing to be hounded by mysterious enemies that left death knives on tables and blasted space ships without warning. It was quite another to see these treacheries coming into focus in the motives of Paul Maddergall and Old Man Zuber. There was some comfort in knowing your own deadliest hates were aimed in the right direction.

Lights played along the fence that surrounded the Zuber yards. Joe gave them a wide berth until the nearness of the coast drew him in closer.

A guard bobbed up from somewhere and shouted, "Hey, who's there? That you, Tom?"

Joe stopped in the shadows and waited. The guard called again, and someone answered from a point farther up the line. The guard was apparently satisfied. Joe could hear the two of them shuffling along through the metal-strewn paths until they met. They fell into a discussion about the moving metals, and Joe slipped along unnoticed.

He was nearing the point where he had left his coat when he heard the low grind of creeping beams.

Lights played across eastern extremity of the yard and down toward the waters of the Atlantic. The guards were watching from various points, obviously baffled.

"There goes another one," a voice shouted from off across the seaward slope.

"Darned if I know what we can do to stop them," someone yelled back. "We've tried everything."

"If this keeps up the Old Man's going to notice."

"They've got a lively gravity pull, that's all. They won't float off too far. Let the Old Man dredge the sea. What the hell."

"He'll be blazin' mad when he sees how his fence is tore out, and that's when we'll get it in the neck. He's losing hundreds of dollars on every beam that crawls off. We'd better report."

Joe moved on more boldly. The guards were too busy watching the action of the big pieces of metal to be aware of trespassers. He reached the spot where he and Dynamo had hidden to eavesdrop. Over the bank, out of the level of the lights, he rummaged around among the warm rocks. Here was the coat, all right, lying right where he had left it.

A shower of dust and sand fell over him as he straightened up, coat in hand. A huge cylindrical beam was slipping out over the bank right above his head.

He jumped back and stumbled. The black mass was riding out like a huge oil tank over an embankment. For a moment he thought it was falling on him. Impulsively he reached up to protect himself, at the same time doing his best to regain his feet.

"There goes another big one," he heard someone shout. "That's one of those two-hundred-footers. Look at that thing crawl."

WITH A GRIND of earth and rocks, the big cylindrical piece moved out like a streamline train shooting off the end of the track. Joe's hand felt the round underbelly of the beam as it skimmed over him. His fingers rubbed against a square metal button that made him think of an electric buzzer. It must have been a key or a lever. He heard something fly open.

Whoosh!

The suction pulled at him. He came off his feet. His shoulder struck the curved edge of what must have been a trap door. The reflected light barely outlined the opening, and that bit of light was all that saved him. The suction pulled at his hair and clothing, but he kicked against the visible edge of the trap door and fell away.

He fell twelve or fifteen feet onto the rocky bank, for by this time the outward movement of the huge metal beam had carried him away from his original footing. As it kept moving it would soon teeter-totter over the bank's edge and then angle down toward the ocean. He rolled to his feet, struck for a stretch of lighted surface, and raced for safety out across the sand.

"Hey, look down there!" one of the guards shouted. "Someone fell out of that big pipe. I saw someone running."

"You're seeing things," someone retorted. "The rocks are rolling."

"Yeah? Do rocks have legs? Don't tell me. Those darn things are inhabited. That's why they crawl. Someone's inside, running the powerhouse."

Another voice in the darkness declared that the Old Man had better come around and get a load of what was happening.

"He's already seen," a guard replied. "He came around this afternoon, him and Mouse Moberly. Now he's got a bad headache and don't want to hear no more about it."

Joe knew he was lucky to get out of range without being pursued, for someone had certainly glimpsed him chasing off into the blackness. He was luckier still to have escaped the draughty pull of the hollow steel beam. It had almost pulled his clothing off of him before he kicked away. It had got his coat.

"Goodbye, letter," he muttered. "I'll never know what it was."

Now with a rip and an earth-shuddering thump, the big beam tilted over the bank like an overweighted teeter-totter, and crushed down over rocks and sand and the remains of the fence. As rigid as a rocket, it slid forward into the sea. The lights of the guard towers followed it, and Joe saw the long splash and heard the roar as it was swallowed up.

High on another bank he lay, applying salve and bandages to his bleeding legs distractedly. All night long the strange movements of metals continued seaward—pieces of all conceivable shapes. He could only lie and wonder what it was all about. He waited and watched, as if in a nightmare. His sore legs rebelled against the trudge back to the bus line; and as long as the big shadowy movements continued from across the slope he was too fascinated to move.

At the first gray of dawn he looked out over the black Atlantic and saw a sight that no man on earth had ever seen before.

CHAPTER FOUR

IT CAME up out of the sea from somewhere about two miles east of the shore. At first it was only a clot of light away out there on the black waters. Joe watched it, wondering what ship it could be, carrying such a powerful searchlight.

The point of light was restless. It turned this way and that, not with the regularity of a beacon, but with a nervous movement. It moved like the eyes of a lost child trying to get his bearings.

Then it began to rise. Out of the dark waters against the gray of the eastern sky it moved upward like a gigantic searchlight on a tower, being pushed up from its submerged base. The tower that supported it widened into a gigantic head. The light of early dawn gleamed on its silvery surface.

In every way it was like a head, Joe thought. A head surmounted by a massive light that shot straight, hard beams out across the black Atlantic. It was like a head in the way it moved. It moved not as a boat glides but as a man walks. As it rose higher, the great dark bulk of its wide shoulders came into view—shoulders with arms that hung down in the water. It was walking shoreward. If it had feet they must be treading the ocean floor; for with its shoreward approach it grew taller and taller. Out of the depths came its vast body, a gigantic chest that tapered down into narrower hips; chest and pelvis and legs of gleaming steel. The long arms swung with the easy gait of its walking, graceful steel fingers silhouetted cleanly against the morning sky.

The sun was rising, and Joe thought the iron monster's headlight must have dimmed a little—until the beam chanced to turn directly on that part of the shore where he lay watching. The brilliance with which every detail of the shoreline was suddenly lighted made Joe feel naked.

The light turned away slowly and Joe's eyes swam. For minutes he had been watching as if hypnotized. Perhaps more than an hour had passed—yes, more than that, he knew, for the morning had turned from darkness to full daylight. And during it all he had lain helpless, as if he had been struck down by a physical blow.

The urgency to get up and run pried at him in vain. He seemed to be experiencing a nightmare that he couldn't break out of. Were other people seeing what he saw? All along the shore for miles in both directions the towering iron monster must be visible.

Where was the great creature going? What did it mean to do? How close to the shore would it come, trudging step by step into the shallower waters? Across the low waves Joe could see the stalking movements of its shadow. The shadow advanced to the piers down the shore and slowly edged over a row of industries around the point of land. People in those far-off apartment buildings, Joe thought, must be awakening with cries of terror. Nearer at hand were a few fishermen's shanties, from which the fishermen had already pushed out to sea. Were their families still sleeping peacefully? What a shock they would have when they looked out at the morning sky.

"It must be hundreds of feet tall," Joe guessed, trying to gauge by a distant lighthouse.

SUDDENLY he was running. He ran, hardly knowing why. It was a dizzy impulse to tell everybody, to shout to the houses up and down the coast, to cry an alarm. But how far would he get on his lame limping legs? He scrambled over the rocks along the sea wall and jogged into an open lane. From some of the huts he could hear the radios blaring. Of course, the coastguardsmen were already shouting it to the world. How silly of him to think that he had anything to tell.

Yet he knew something about it that they didn't know. Again he stood, peering into the distant east. "Born under the sea," he said aloud. Tall and black and terrible against the white sky, it walked like a man. "Born under the sea," he repeated.

"Born under the sea," the voice of a girl spoke quietly.

That was the first he had realized anyone was near him. But people were coming out of their houses now, pointing and shouting. And so Joe was hardly surprised to discover that someone was standing nearby.

"I watched the metal parts move down into the ocean," Joe said, hardly looking at her. He pointed. "See those long arms? Those were beams of steel lying on the ground up at Zuber's."

"Who put them together?" the girl asked.

"They put themselves together."

"But what is it? What's it for?"

"Look at it move. It's a giant of power. It's hundreds of feet tall: See how small that lighthouse is?"

"What's it for? I don't understand." The girl repeated her plaintive question several times. Joe was so intent upon watching that he hardly heard her. Then he felt her tugging at his sleeve, and knew she was asking the question in fright. "What's it going to do? I'm afraid."

He turned to look at her. She was a girl of eighteen or nineteen. Fear shone in her dark liquid eyes. She had evidently hurried out of the house in her dressing gown. Her dark hair hung loosely over her shoulders. With one hand she held the collars of her gown at her throat. She was barefoot.

"Look, the boats are going out to it," she said. "It must be something the government has built—though why would they build such a monster?"

Joe watched the coast guard cutters ploughing out from shore. He could imagine the men on board looking up at the big tower of steel hovering over them.

"Say, they're plenty nervy," he muttered. "They're taking an awful chance. Suppose that thing would stumble and fall."

"Is it alive?"

"I wish I could answer all your questions. It's just a great big mechanism, I can tell you that. And it was born at sea, because I watched it go in, piece by piece, and I saw it come out walking upright. And I can guess a couple of other guesses. It's just the first one. There'll be more."

"Oh."

"I'm not trying to scare you. I just happen to know that more metal has crept into the ocean than we see in that one monster. There could be another, any hour of any day."

"It looks so—so hideous. Do you think it could possibly be harmless?"

The girl was standing so close beside him he was tempted to slip his arm around her. She gave a glad little cry. "Oh, look. It's giving them a signal."

THE GREAT dark hand of the steel monster was slowly rising as the nearest boat moved across its path. Joe held his breath hopefully. The giant arm raised—yes, it was surely a signal of friendship. The open hand was being lifted—

Then suddenly the great steel fist clenched and the arm came down like a hammer. The fist struck the boat squarely.

"What happened?" the girl cried. "Something went wrong. It hit the boat. Where is it? Where's the boat?"

"The boat's gone," Joe said coldly.

"What a dreadful accident. Oh, that's terrible. It just struck down, like a club—"

"It was no accident," Joe said quietly. The breath went out of him. "Look...look..."

The massive man of steel bent toward two other boats that had followed the first. The huge searchlight on its head turned down upon one of them. Now both boats were turning about, powering for a quick getaway. But the big iron hand came down on the end of one of them.

It sliced down sidewise like an ax. The glancing blow made the boat leap out of the water. Quick as a lightning flash the other big mechanical hand swung and caught it in midair. It might have been a celluloid toy. The big steel fingers lifted it to a level with the massive head, and the blaze of the searchlight turned full on it. Then the steel fingers squeezed with a death grip. In a moment the faint echoes of wood and metal crunching came across the waters to Joe's ears.

The hand opened. The wreckage fell from it, struck the water, and sank. The big searchlight turned to look for the third boat, and the wide waves went out from the Iron Man's towering form as it continued to plod along through the ocean.

The girl was crying. Her head was against Joe's shoulder. What would happen, she was asking through her sobs. If more of these monsters were on their way, what would happen? Would everything be destroyed?

"Listen, friend," Joe said quietly, holding her tight in his arms. "I can't tell you what's going to happen. Nobody can. Nobody knows. But I can give you some good advice."

She looked up at him and drew away a little. "I'm sorry, acting like this."

"You don't need to apologize. After what we've just seen, we're both scared out of our senses and we'd just as well admit it. As soon as the radios get this out to the people, the whole country's going to be in a panic. I hope you didn't have a father or a brother out on one of those boats."

She shook her head. "I only have a father. He used to be a fisherman." She pointed to the nearest house. "He's in there—bedfast."

"That's bad." He regarded her with interest. "That must be a big job for you."

"We're getting along so far. I work. It's time I was at the

restaurant now. I work over on the highway. But I can't go this morning, and leave him—"

"Don't you worry about any restaurant job. The way that thing's moving, they'll never open the doors this morning. Look, people are already getting out."

DOWN THE shoreline people, screeching like crazed birds, were loading into their cars and tearing out. A vision of mad traffic jams and stampeding mobs came to Joe's mind.

"You were going to advise—"

"You'd better not lose any time," Joe said crisply. "Can you get your father on to a bus? You don't have a car, do you?"

"A pick-up that Dad used to run. I drive it a little. But where would I go?"

"Inland, anywhere. Anywhere away from the coast and the city. That monster was born in water, and he might stick to the ocean or the streams. Anyway you'll be in less danger inland. Come on, I'll help you get started."

He thought she was going to faint, she looked so pale, passing her hand over her forehead. Then she gave him a smile. "I'm sorry to be such a weakling. But I feel so—so helpless. I don't know where we can go. And we haven't any money. Less than a dollar. Today would be payday. If I could go to the restaurant—"

"No time for that." Joe jerked out his billfold. "Here, I can spare part of this. Here's twenty-three dollars." He forced it into her hands. "Now, no time to waste. Let's get that car of yours into action."

"I've never taken money from a stranger," she said between breaths as they ran toward the house. "But I seem to know you…I knew your voice when I heard you say…born under the sea…I guess I've heard you on television…was it yesterday morning?"

Joe took the car keys and ran around to the dilapidated

little truck in the back yard. It sputtered twice, then roared into life. He swung around to the front step. A flurry of talk, groans from the old man, a scurrying of steps, a bouncing of two battered old suitcases, and within minutes they were locking the door and helping the weak, sick old man down to the car.

"I'll drive you to the other side of the city," Joe said.

"Father," the girl said, as they settled together in the single seat, "this is Joe Kane, the boy you liked so well on the television program yesterday morning...and my name is Mary."

"We have relatives in the mountains," the old man spoke painfully. "We'll go there."

A wide shadow moved over them like a fast-moving cloud approaching somewhere from the east. Joe steered the car through the gate and down the lane. As soon as he got onto the highway his foot went down to the floorboard.

CHAPTER FIVE

COMING back into the city after escorting Mary and her father safely to the highway beyond, Joe wondered if he was behaving like a man returning to a burning building. All the way back, on foot, by bus, and by taxi, he headed into swarms of outbound traffic. It was like a wartime evacuation. Perhaps it was the beginning of war.

He was now many miles west of the coast where the Iron Man was marching. Radios blared the latest news from all directions. From overhead scouting planes with loudspeakers called down at the stampeding crowds to take their time.

"Don't rush...don't rush. The danger is many miles away. Keep in order...obey all traffic signals. The danger is not near this area."

Well out of the so-called danger area Joe entered one of the city's great public buildings and took an elevator down to the underground offices.

"I've got to see Commander Doyle."

"I'm afraid not, sir." The secretary was polite but firm. "The commander is not receiving unofficial visitors."

"I had an appointment. I called yesterday. They said I might see him today."

"I'm sorry, sir. All appointments are off."

"But this is urgent. This is—"

"Talk with the man in the blue uniform," the secretary said, and gave Joe a wave of dismissal.

The man in the blue uniform had been placed to handle just such eager callers as Joe.

"Sorry, buddy, it can't be done."

"I've got to see him. It's about the emergency."

"Yeah? Did you come in off the streets? Did you hear those sirens out there? That's all about the emergency. Planes going over? Tanks moving down to the shore? That's what they're all about, buddy—the emergency. Now I know the commander would be tickled pink to have a nice chummy visit with you, but you're just one little squeak in a great big roar. So—"

"Listen, sir," Joe tried hard to be polite while he was burning up, "I happen to have information—inside information. If I can see Commander Doyle for just five minutes—"

For a moment Joe thought the big man in blue was weakening as he turned to another official. "Still keeping count, George? Here's another man that swears he's got inside information."

"Thirty-seven," said the other official with a wink. "By noon we'll have a hundred. Why didn't these inside information crackbrains come in yesterday? Why wait till the world's getting smashed to hell?"

Joe's voice got angry. "Listen, I did try yesterday. They told me today. You'll find it on the books. The name is Joe Kane."

The officer sneered. "Joe Kane, Joe Doakes, Joe

Blowhard—"

"It's Joe Kane." Joe was fairly on the desk that blocked his way. The officer gave him a push back on his heels.

"It's all the same to me, buddy. If I let you inside that door, you'd come right out on your ear. I'm protecting you. I'm telling you nice like a mother." Then the man in blue stopped talking and fastened his eyes on something across the room. Joe looked. Everyone in the room looked. The fifteen-foot television screen brought in the outside world like a picture window. The room grew quiet as the crowd watched. Joe saw at a glance what was happening. The big iron monster was moving slowly up into the bay.

"He's got a mania for boats," someone muttered.

"He put the kayo on a big ocean liner just outside the harbor," another commented. "Pounded it like a trip hammer till it sank."

"I'm getting out of here. He could uproot this whole city if he once got started."

SOME OF the spectators made for the door; others preferred the underground offices to the peril of going up on the surface. Every minute or so the voices of the newscasters would call out the Iron Man's position. Persons who were not in the area of immediate danger were urged to stay where they were. As yet the streets of the city were safe. But it was feared that a panic flight might attract the monster's attention. "Stay out of the traffic... Stay where you are... Do not leave your building unless your area is ordered to evacuate..."

Under the heavy voice of the announcer were the low excited hisses of those watching the screen. Another boat!

"He's after that tugboat. There it goes. He's got it."

The luckless tugboat failed to make it to the shore. The Iron Man reached for it. The great steel fingers of death closed over it. Out of the cacophony came the sound of the crush. The splintered mass splashed into the water. The telescopic lens brought a close-up of the water. There might be numerous survivors swimming for the shore. The television camera spotted one. He was dragging an arm, bloody, twisted. A white patch across his head showed were his skull had been sliced. He was crying with pain, yet swimming like mad. Then the big steel fingertip smashed down across his body.

"Where'd he go?"

"Down."

"He looked like someone I knew once."

"It could have been any of us."

The television camera played over the empty waters for a moment and then began to move upward. The close-up rose slowly, taking in the full height of the towering steel form. The plates of metal that formed the head were fitted with the same monotonous regularity as those of the expansive chest. The face gave no expression.

"It's a machine. That's all you can make of it."

"That face has the look of the very devil, if you ask me."

"It hasn't any look at all. It's just a machine."

"The ferry boat!" someone gasped. "That's the boat my girl friend always comes over on."

"It's turning back…It's trying to, anyway. Or is it drifting?"

"Why did they ever let it leave the shore? They should have known better. "

"Look, he's going after it. Just two long steps and he's right over it. He's going to get it, all right."

"There's no one on it—it's empty. It must be a trick."

The screen brought the scene up close. The steel giant's hands came down upon the boat and lifted it out of the water. They started to tear it like a pack of cards. There was a great flash of fire.

"I told you it was a trick!" someone cried. "They had the darn thing loaded with explosives. It's blown up."

THE CLOUD of smoke cleared, and the big metal hand could be seen brushing off the splinters of exploded wreckage. Burning debris hissed into the water. The big creature of Venus metal stalked on slowly, apparently unscathed.

"Here comes the Air force!" was the next hopeful cry from the crowd around the screen.

Bomb-laden flying ships whipped into the picture at high speed. Bombs dropped, and the explosions rocked the earth and the sea. And when the smoke cleared, the Iron Man stood where he had stood before, unshaken.

"Here come four fast ones."

"Yes, and he's got a weapon ready for them."

The planes cut across the picture like bullets. The Iron Man reached to his side. A weapon hung there. It fairly leaped into his hand. Its colored barrels gleamed in the sun. The hand rose to take aim.

"Smoke. They're trying to blind him with smoke."

The watchers around the screen went wild with sudden hope. Great clouds of black smoke boiled around the towering monster. The four planes had fired smoke bombs. Out of the mass the Iron Man's pistol flashed.

"He's shooting at himself. He can't see! He's aiming at himself!"

"He's aiming at the smoke around him."

The pistol fanned out a spray of blue light. The smoke rolled into it. It might have been a vacuum, the way the cloud rushed in. A moment later the air was crystal clear.

The four planes came screaming back. The pistol turned on them. Instead of a blue spray, it shot a pencil-thin ray of yellow. Zip. Zip. Two lines of yellow jumped from one of the pistol barrels. Two planes were struck with mathematical precision. They burst into flames. Zip. Plane number three caught the deadly ray and exploded. Zip. The ray went its length but fell short. Plane number four rode away on the wings of luck.

"What next?"

"More planes. I hear them. My heavens, this is suicide!"

While the whole room was engrossed, Joe quietly slipped through the unguarded door that led to Commander Doyle's office.

In the midst of a whirl of orders to his battery of secretaries, the tall steely-eyed uniformed commander turned to face Joe.

"Who are you and what do you want?" the commander snapped.

CHAPTER SIX

JOE HANDED Commander Doyle a card. "I'm Joe Kane, and I have some very important information. You need my help."

The Commander stared at him dubiously. Joe's voice had quavered. He was afraid—not afraid of facing the commander, but afraid that some trifling error would cause him to fall down, now that the moment had come to tell his story. This chance would surely never come again. The commander waited.

"I know something about the plot, sir. Two of our own men are scheming to use Venus help to overthrow..."

"Stop right where you are, young man. I've heard that tale every day for weeks. Everyone is accusing everyone else. Any man with an enemy wants to tell me privately that his enemy is linked with the Venus killers. "

"Yes, sir, but what I've overheard makes me very sure—"

"Two men, you say? Who are they?"

"Paul Maddergall and—"

"Maddergall, the investigator? Hold on, young man. Aren't you the same Joe Kane who had a round with Maddergall yesterday morning?"

"Yes sir, but—"

"I can see right through your grievance and it sounds just

like dozens of others. Who's your other man?"

"Zuber. He and Maddergall are plotting together—"

"Who let you in here anyway?"

Joe swallowed hard. "I—just came in. That is—"

"I'm sorry to be curt with you, young man, but I'm not the world court, you know. If you gather any evidence against your fellow citizens that will hold water, take it to the proper authorities—"

"But I knew I could trust you. Commander Doyle, listen to me. I know where that Iron Man came from. And Zuber knows. It's come from pieces of Venus steel he's shipped in. They've slipped into the sea and they've pulled together automatically, and somehow—"

Now all at once Doyle's fine face was alight with interest. He regarded Joe from head to foot as if taking his measure. He said, "Go on, Kane, I'm listening."

"We watched the pieces slide into the sea—my friend Dinkins and I. We heard Zuber and his assistant talking about it. They didn't know we were listening. That's, when they talked about Maddergall being in with them—"

"No, get back to the Iron Man.

What you've just said fits with stories I've had from several other sources. There's no doubt about the metals creeping away and locking together in a pre-planned fashion. But tell me this, Kane, do you have any evidence that Zuber knows how this Iron Man works?"

"No."

"Do you think he does know?"

Joe frowned. "No, he doesn't know. He was as surprised as anyone else to know the stuff contained some kind of internal power units."

"That's what I thought. In other words he doesn't know a thing that would help us defeat this monster with one quick stroke?"

"No."

"Then I would say he doesn't deserve to be linked with

the Venus killers. He may fall victim to this senseless destruction any hour the same as the rest of us."

Joe wanted to say that Zuber and Maddergall had simply let their own plan get out of hand—which didn't make them any less guilty of treason against the earth. But before he could say it, Commander Doyle carried him off in the other direction.

"The one desperate need of the moment, Joe Kane, is an understanding of the operation of that steel giant. It defies our bombs, and obviously it's paving the way for an attack from the killers."

"Yes, sir."

"Have you any information regarding the secret of its operation?"

"No, sir."

"If you know of anyone bold enough to get that secret, I'll be glad to supply a ship and fuel or anything else needed."

"I'd be glad to try, sir," Joe said. "My friend Dynamo will probably help me."

"You realize, don't you, that any ship that flies within range of that steel brute gets sudden death?"

Joe nodded. "My brother Lanny got sudden death yesterday. That gives me plenty of reason to put all I've got into this fight."

The commander asked a secretary to make out a blank order for whatever Joe Kane might need. He offered Joe a handshake and good wishes. Then he touched a button and a moment later the man in the blue uniform appeared.

"This is Joe Kane," Commander Doyle said. "Any time he comes in asking to see me—"

"I bounce him out on his ear—yes sir," the eager officer said.

"You conduct him back to this office to see me," the commander said, "with due respect...good luck, Kane."

CHAPTER SEVEN

"THAT'S EIGHT times we've circled him," Dynamo said as they banked their plane in a direction out of range of danger. "And I'll swear we don't know a thing we didn't know two hours ago. We know he kills if we get in range. We know he's standing in the middle of the bay threatening the cities all around. We know he's got eyes in the back of his head. We know he can take all the smoke screens we brew up, and melt them away with one blue puff from his pistol. What else do we know?"

"We're trying. We're working on it," Joe said gloomily. "We're not running away, are we? We're not quitting."

"In some ways he's like a man," Dynamo said. "He works awhile, then he gets fed up with it all and he rests awhile. He gets fed up with resting and he works awhile. His work happens to be killing."

Joe looked back through the summer clouds. The monster had advanced leisurely up the river a short distance, smashing any boats that caught his attention. He towered high above the lower clouds, well above the tops of the tallest buildings.

"If he's enough like a man, we ought to find a way of outwitting him."

"But then again he's not like a man," Dynamo said. "He doesn't eat and he doesn't drink. So far as you can tell, he doesn't have any heart or soul. His heart is all steel and his soul has gone to the devil."

"I've been thinking along those lines," Joe said. "There's more of downright cruelty in him than you ever saw in any man. You take a seasoned killer—he may put a blowtorch to his enemy, but he wouldn't necessarily harm a child—not unless he was mad. But this monster never pulls a punch for anyone. You saw it yourself on television—that party of young kids along the shoreline. He reached over and caught them on the sidewalk and hammered them till there wasn't anything left but stains."

"Why?"

"That's what I'm asking. Why?" Joe groaned. "Heaven knows there's no human motive back of a thing like that. It just does not make sense—not unless the Venus killers have

THE IRON MEN OF VENUS

By
Don Wilcox

Interior Artwork by Ed Valigursky

wound him up, somehow, and turned him loose to go on a terrorizing spree—"

"Just to soften us up for what's coming," Dynamo said. "I reckon that's it."

THEY CIRCLED back, watching him through the telescope. He was beginning to act up again, and this time he directed his blows at the buildings above the shoreline. Standing knee deep in the water, he clung to his pistol with one hand. With the other he hammered at the tops of a row of buildings. He tore away a section of a huge steel bridge and used it as a club. Right down the line he went, striking one big building after another. Fires broke out in his wake.

"I don't see many people," Dynamo said. "Looks like they've left it all to him."

"They've had plenty of warning to go underground. But you know how warnings are. Some folks always think they can outsmart the authorities. He's probably mangling a few bodies every time he lowers that fist."

"Look out, Joe, we're getting pretty close."

The Iron Man heard them coming, that was plain. He straightened suddenly and fired his pistol. The line of yellow came straight toward them, widening into a blot that was blinding. Joe throttled for a swift climb.

"We're gone," Dynamo groaned.

"Not if we're still here to tell about it," Joe said. They pulled away, knowing it had been a close call. They couldn't have been fast enough to dodge the ray, they knew that; it had just fallen short, that was all. Dynamo dug into his coat and brought out two bottles of grape pop, ready chilled.

"Have a cool drink," Dynamo said, "and then tell me this. How are you going to outwit a thing—man or machine— that's twice as quick as you are and a helluva lot more deadly?"

"It's like Commander Doyle said. There's got to be a key somewhere."

"You mean the key they wound the darn thing up with?"

Joe glanced to catch the ironic light in Dynamo's eye. They both saw the absurdity of trying to compare the Iron Man with some complex mechanical toy. There couldn't be anything "set" in such complicated fashion that it would invariably come through with all those quick human reactions.

"It's responding to a human being's will," Joe said. "And the folks that are running it are either inside it or close about. For all we know, the whole military staff of the Venus killers may be camped right up there in its big iron head, looking out in all directions for a chance to make trouble."

Again they made a wide circle around, studying the Iron Man's head through the telescope. Joe believed that a fine photograph would show apertures on all sides for alert human eyes to look through.

That was the one theory he and Dynamo brought back with them when they descended to the landing field. They taxied to a stop and sat in the plane discussing it. Dynamo wasn't very well satisfied with the reasoning.

"Somehow, Joe, I just can't see them acting together that quick and that precise. Here. I'll show you why." Dynamo dug into his coat and came up with a little square box with a screen across the top. Inside were his three pet mice. "Look, what have I got here, Joe?"

"Three mice."

"I've got the Iron Man's head, like you describe it, with the whole damn military staff inside. They're all peeking out separate windows on the lookout for trouble. Right on their toes, you betcha. All of a sudden I blow off a firecracker, let's say. The blast is so close they all jump at once. So what happens? Do they stop and take a vote on what they're gonna do about it? Do they say: let Bill decide this time what we do? There's no time for that. There's no time to think, much less talk. There's just time to act, that quick. And you tell me how these three mice, surrounded by fifty thousand levers and push buttons, all happen to jump for pushbutton number twenty-two thousand five hundred and ninety-nine— or whatever the case may be? Tell me, Joe, how is that?"

Joe nodded slowly. "Those mice look hungry, Dynamo. We'd better stop at a store and get them some cheese."

Dynamo reached into his coat. Just by merest chance, I happen to have some cheese."

Joe looked across to the fiery horizon where the tall dark iron figure stood towering above the burning buildings. The figure stood motionless with arms dropped casually at his sides.

"Now what's he up to?" Dynamo asked.

"It could be lunch time up there too, you know. Something tells me the whole Venus Killer staff is up there in that fellow's hollow dome, munching on cheese sandwiches."

"Cut it out, Joe. You're making fun of me. Just because these mice are gobbling cheese doesn't prove—"

"The only way to prove what's inside that monster is to get inside and see for ourselves. Dynamo, have you got the nerve?"

"Lead the way," Dynamo said.

CHAPTER EIGHT

THE MAN in the blue uniform in Commander Doyle's reception room gave them a skeptical eye, but his tone was one of respect.

"Yes, gentlemen. Right this way, please," and he

conducted them back to the commander's office.

The commander was having coffee, dictating to two stenographers, and keeping a nervous eye on the television screen all at the same time. He greeted Joe and Dynamo briskly and asked them to sit down.

"You almost got shot down up there, Kane. The yellow ray came within yards of you. The folks around the television were screaming for you to get out of range. We don't want any careless casualties. Did you accomplish anything at all? Have you any new ideas? We're stumped, are we? Even the big guns have failed to stagger that monster.

"Sir, we'd like to try to climb up inside him. A little well-placed destruction—"

"My theory exactly. A small handful of explosives at some key spot—perhaps the base of the electric brain, or whatever the devil it is that makes him function. The fact is, Kane, we already have two suicide squads at work on the plans. They'll go to work if they can get an angle."

"Maybe we could join them," Dynamo suggested. "Or beat them to the punch."

"Didn't you work all night last night, Dinkins?" the commander asked sharply.

"Yes, sir, come to think of it."

"And you, Kane?"

"I spent the night watching."

"I strongly advise that you both get some rest. You look a bit exhausted. Go home and sleep. Call back at four in the morning. If the squads haven't found their way to kayo the monster by that time, you boys have the green light."

"Thank you, sir." They started off.

"Oh, Kane," the commander called, beckoning. "May I have a private word with you before you go?"

Dynamo gave a puzzled grin and bowed out. Joe came back to Doyle's desk. He took a chair and waited. The commander shuffled through some of the papers on his desk as if looking for a memo. He was a bit embarrassed over something he wanted to say, Joe thought.

"I hate to give anyone the job of climbing inside that Iron Man," he said casually.

"We've asked for it."

"It does sound like a suicide assignment, doesn't it?"

"It could be. There must be some Venus killers somewhere inside the Iron Man—probably up in his head-"

"And now I remember what I wanted to ask you," Commander Doyle broke in as if he had lost the trail of Joe's speculations. "What can you tell me about your brother, Ruppert Kane?"

"Ruppert?" Joe's eyes widened. At a time like this why should they stop to discuss his brother Ruppert? "I don't follow you. Is Ruppert here? Have you seen him?"

"I've no intention of embarrassing you, Joe." The commander turned to one of the secretaries. "Where did you find that coffee, Miss Garnett? Get a cup for Mr. Kane, please...there, Joe, don't let the question worry you. You see, the minute this trouble from Venus thickened, the earth governments began to send notes of protest to the Venus Storm Colony. Now nothing would suit those boys better than to try to pin the responsibility on their earth friends, shall we say. Is it your belief that your brother Ruppert was a friend of the Venus killers?"

"Not exactly a friend," Joe said. "He was more of an interested observer. He's done a lot of travelling. Different types of people are his hobby."

"Do you think he has carried any hatred toward the earth and its people?"

"Oh, no. Why should he?"

"He was disappointed in love once, wasn't he?"

"Well, yes, I guess that went pretty deep." Joe met Doyle's eyes. "Yes, he was in love with someone who later married Paul Maddergall."

"But you don't think that disappointment turned into a

powerful hatred?"

"No...emphatically *no*," Joe insisted. "He was a very mild person, tender-hearted. He could hardly kill a fly, he was so-so soft. This was his worst fault, if you can call it that."

"Well, thank you, Joe, that answers my question. It just goes to prove that those replies we receive from Venus aren't to be trusted at all."

"Will I see Ruppert again?"

"I don't know, son."

"But do you know where he is?"

"After what you've told me—no, I haven't the slightest idea where he is. He may not even be involved in this trouble at all. He probably isn't. Please just forget that I even mentioned him."

LONG AFTER their conference was over, Joe kept recounting what had been said. The more he studied the matter, the less he could make of it. But one word of parting advice he took from Commander Doyle, and passed it along to Dynamo as well. They should attempt nothing before tomorrow. Since the Iron Man had apparently spent himself for the day, Joe and Dynamo would do well to treat themselves to a night's sleep before undertaking their daring action.

"Anything I can help you with?" Dynamo asked as they were nearing the apartment-house entrance. It was natural that he would be curious about the private talk Joe and the commander had had.

"He asked me about Ruppert. Same old story, only now it's the Venus killers trying to hang something on him."

Dynamo suppressed a groan as if resolving to say nothing.

"I know," Joe said gloomily. "Ruppert's a made-to-order stooge. Back in college days he was the one they blamed for leading the cow into the dean's bedroom during the milk shortage."

"Did he do it?"

"He didn't even know there was a milk shortage. He was off in a museum somewhere droning over the butterfly collection. Chances are, he's off in some remote regions of Jupiter this very night, studying the habits of the natives."

Dynamo shrugged. "I don't know why he had to be born into your family."

In the apartment building they descended to their floor, eighteen stories below the surface, and ambled out of the elevator wearily.

"They're inspecting again," the elevator man said casually. "In fact, I think he's in your room now."

"He, who?"

"The man that was here before, checking on our underground space," Joe scowled. He turned back to the elevator man. "Wait a minute. I don't get you."

"It's the emergency," the elevator man said importantly. "Don't you know, people on the surface are being packed in with the people that live down in. They're going around measuring the square feet of space, so they'll know—"

"No, no, no," Joe said. "They don't go around measuring. They look at the floor plan, that's all. You mean to tell me you've let some person into our apartment? Did you?"

"Well, I wasn't going to," the elevator man began to hedge. "But he had his papers. He showed me. When he was here before—"

"Here before? When? What day?"

"Must have been about two days ago. You can ask him yourself. He's in there now."

"Quick, Dynamo," Joe said. "This has a phony sound."

THEY HURRIED to the apartment door. It started to open as we neared, but instantly closed. With drawn pistols they moved in, cautiously at first, then darting fast into the room. The lights showed an empty room. Footsteps sounded with a light scampering toward the airshaft in the next room.

"Same visitor." Dynamo pointed to the study tables where he and Joe kept their papers. On each table stood a gleaming red Venus knife, pointing up.

The clatter of the air vent told them the desperate prowler meant to get out of the place unseen.

"Come back and fight!" Joe called out. "Come back and show your face."

The slats of the air vent clattered to one side. The slight, gray-clad form of a man was disappearing that way.

"Fool. He'll never climb eighteen floors inside that."

Crack! A pistol shot sounded in the shaft. Heedless of the danger, Joe stuck his head and shoulders through the opening, flung an arm upward into the darkness, and caught the runaway by the ankle. The fellow's pistol must have slipped from his hand. Joe heard it clattering down along the brick shaft to the bottom of the well.

Joe clung to the fellow's ankle and pulled.

"Come easy or fall to a quick death," Joe said.

A brittle tin-like voice snapped an answer. "I've signaled my men. You'd better let go. They're on their way. For your own good you'd better let go."

"You're coming in if I have to tear you apart," Joe swore, and he put his muscles to the task. Whatever the fellow was hanging to, his hands gave way. He gave a savage little cry, and came with a jerk. Joe tumbled him into the room. Dynamo was on him, removing everything from extra pistol to fountain pen. Then he and Joe stood back to study the little fellow's bruised face under the light.

"The wall kind of battered you up," Dynamo said, "but I think I know you."

The small man glared defiantly. He glanced at the airshaft as though he expected a squad of bodyguards to march in to his rescue.

"Yeah, sure we know him," Joe said. "This is Mouse

Moberly, the brain of the Zuber works."

"Right," said Dynamo. "One of my bosses."

"Thank you for the compliments, gentlemen," the battered little man said, dusting his hands. "This is all a mistake that I can explain—"

"You bet it's a mistake. Just dropped in for a friendly visit, did you? Left your calling cards sticking up on our tables. Nice and friendly." Dynamo's tone was rich with sarcasm.

Joe spoke with a fury that ran deep. "Now we know who planted the warning for my brother Lanny. And it's a fair guess that you were back of Senator Droondair's murder too."

"Sort of building yourself for the revolution you and Zuber aim to put over, is that it?" Dynamo said. "Mouse Moberly, Grand Mogul of the metal monsters. A mighty man is Mouse Moberly—under a magnifying glass."

"Talk, gentlemen. Say whatever you please. In five minutes you'll both be dead."

"In five minutes," Dynamo said, "you'll be safe in the arms of the law." He started for the telephone.

"Wait, Dynamo," Joe said. "I think I have a better idea. This man is good at climbing up airshafts. He might be good at climbing up the legs of the Iron Man. We'll take him along as a mascot. If we get into a tight place—"

THE DOORBELL rang, and at the same moment Joe thought he heard more sounds coming from the airshaft. Dynamo reached into his coat and brought out a short piece of rope. They tied Mouse hand and foot and carried him to the door. The bell rang again.

"Now, Mouse," Joe said in a low voice, "you're a big boss and you like to have your orders obeyed without any back-talk." His hand was over the little man's mouth. Mouse Moberly was fairly purple with rage. "We're the boss now. You're smart enough to do as we say. Tell the men it's all clear, they can come in. The door's unlocked."

Mouse batted his eyes and tried to nod. Joe let him talk. Mouse spoke sullenly.

"Come on in, Winkler. It's all clear. The door's unlocked."

Winkler opened the door and walked in, a thickset man with protruding eyes and a gravel voice. "What happened? Where's Craddle? What's the matter, are you—ugh!"

Joe stepped up to plant a pistol in Winkler's ribs. Dynamo produced the needed rope, and Winkler was made helpless.

A moment later at the airshaft Joe heard the low, hollow call. "Mouse...Mouse...are you coming up, Mouse?"

Joe whispered his order to the well-tamed Mouse Moberly. "Tell him to get to the elevator and come down. Tell him you need him down here."

Ten minutes later the three prowlers sat in discomfort in three living room chairs. Dynamo stood nearby, playing idly with three red knives. Joe paced the floor, talking like a sergeant with three raw recruits on his hands.

"Now, Mouse—Craddle—Winkler—I've gone over the details, and if you're smart you know there can't be any slip-ups. This job calls for experienced prowlers who know how to climb. I'll wear a headpiece with three ray-pencils attached, one for each of you. I've used them before on troubleshooting jobs. They're like bloodhounds on your trail, and they're instant death if you make a false move. Any questions? Go to sleep, then. We start at four o'clock in the morning."

CHAPTER NINE

JOE SLEPT fitfully. All through the night the news flashes sounded quietly from the radio at his bed. He arose at three thirty. The giant monster of metal had paced back and forth through the harbor until three, the newscaster said.

No destruction, however, had taken place during the night. "The Iron Man is temporarily at rest...he has crouched down on one elbow...he is resting on the area of rubble where he destroyed buildings a few hours ago...efforts to communicate with him, either by radio or by signal, have failed completely...yet the theories persist that he has behaved with human intelligence...his path of destruction has presented a strange pattern that defies analysis...he chose to destroy several public buildings not far from the shore...he crushed the fine new interplanetary museum..."

That would be a shock to Ruppert, Joe thought, for the new museum had been one of Ruppert's favorite haunts.

"...He moved down one row of buildings, smashing each one in turn...until he came to a certain gambling den with a very bad reputation...this he passed over."

Dynamo, also listening, shook his sleepy head. "If I've had any suspicions of your brother Ruppert, I apologize. He couldn't possibly have any influence with the Venus killers if they passed over the gambling dens."

"You remember?"

"I remember there was nothing Ruppert hated worse than gambling. He was hipped on the subject. If he had had an iron fist the size of that monster's, he'd have pulverized every gambling house in the country."

"Thank you," Joe said.

"For what?"

"For saying something fair about my older brother. He's a perfectly swell person—just a little different from other folks. The girl he almost married thought he was a great guy. But don't you see what's happened?"

"You mean Maddergall?"

"Yes. Maddergall smears him with suspicion, and other folks pick it up. The Venus killers need a scapegoat so they answer Commander Doyle's notes and try to make him think our trouble comes from one of our own men—Ruppert. The bad reputation started with one malicious lie, and look where it's got. Even you, my best friend, have begun to talk like Ruppert is something poison."

"I didn't mean to." Dynamo offered his hand. "I'll never say another word against him as long as I live. It's a promise."

THEY CUT the handshake short as the radio announced the time. They called Commander Doyle and received the word they needed from his office. They awakened their three well-bound recruits, untied their feet, and marched them to the elevator, out the door, and into a taxi.

Twenty minutes later the five of them were moving gingerly up the long horizontal steel beam that formed the lower left leg of the Iron Man.

Winkler and Craddle moved sluggishly at the head of the line. They yammered like whipped truants. They wanted firearms. Joe wouldn't even let them have a club. They complained that their recently bound wrists were too weak for climbing. But the sort of sympathy they got from Dynamo didn't encourage them to talk.

"If you slip back," Dynamo said, "I'll catch you on one of these Venus death knives. I've got three, compliments of Mouse Moberly and Company."

"If you think that was my idea," Mouse spat, "you're badly mistaken. I'm just a pawn in this game."

"That ain't what you told us," Winkler called back.

"Shut your head," Mouse snapped.

"Get on, get on, you're stalling," Joe ordered.

The big monster of metal was lying quietly, propped up on one elbow. The rower beam of the leg was resting at an easy angle of approximately thirty degrees. This position, together with the aid of the magnetic grips that the men wore on their shoes, made the climbing no difficult trick. They had begun at the Iron Man's ankles, which rested in the water, their approach having been made by boat.

When they ascended toward the knee, Joe realized that a

bad moment was ahead. The position of the Iron Man was such that the march from the knee joint to the pelvis would be downhill. Since Winkler, Craddle and Mouse were in the lead, they would get the benefit of the downhill trail first. If they saw their opportunity in time they might race away, out of range, before Joe could cross the knee.

He tried to crowd close on their heels. Mouse slipped, fell forward, and acted hurt. He limped.

"Move along. Move along."

"I cracked my arm."

"You don't walk on your arm. Move on. Faster. Faster."

THE OTHER two men were already at the knee. They scrambled over, and the next moment they were out of sight somewhere on the other side. Joe glanced to the shore, all of sixty feet below. They wouldn't chance a jump-off here, but if they got down to those narrow steel hips, out of range, they might make their escape. He hurried Mouse over the big slippery knee joint, and then he saw. The other two men were making a run for it.

"Stop! Stop or I'll cut you down!"

They were already out of range and they knew it. The pencil rays on his headpiece spat two lines of death, like tracer bullets in the early morning twilight. Their light sent reflected gleams along half the length of the Iron Man's upper leg. Winkler and Craddle were never touched.

"They're gone," Dynamo muttered, close behind Joe. He fired two pistol shots. The man, untouched, leaped the gap toward the wide band of copper-colored metal that circled the hips like a strap.

Flash! The copper band met them with a wave of purple fire. Joe saw them move weirdly. They had landed without a fall, but they had been automatically electrocuted. They rolled up in convulsive movements that ended in death.

The great iron monster stirred slightly. Joe, Dynamo and Mouse clung tight, watching. They saw the bodies of

Winkler and Craddle slip like stuffed sacks and across the hips to the ground. The Iron Man stirred as if to find a more comfortable position, and rolled over on them. Mouse turned back to face Joe with a look of horror in his eyes.

Dynamo said, "Nothing like that ever happened in an air shaft, I reckon."

"Take me back," Mouse said. "Get me out of here."

"You mean you don't want to follow them?" Joe said. "It's a good thing we brought you boys along. That might have happened to us. All right, Mouse, take it calm. You're still leading the way, only we're changing the direction."

"We're going back?" Mouse said eagerly.

"Is your bad arm troubling you too much?"

"It's all right."

They marched back down toward the ankle. Dynamo's eyes expressed curiosity, but he waited for Joe to call the play.

"We're going to try a hunch," Joe said. "Unless I'm mistaken, we'll bump into a trap door somewhere down this way."

They padded along the lower extremity of the leg where it disappeared in the shallow water. Joe swept his bare arm back and forth over the metal surface and presently he found what he was looking for.

"Here it is, Dynamo. This gadget that looks like a steel wart. You touch it and it buzzes like an electric buzzer, and everything flies in, you and I and Mouse, all together. Move this way a little."

"Get me out of this," Mouse said. "I've had enough. I'll do whatever you say, but get me out of this."

"All set?" Joe asked, "Hold tight to Mouse, Dynamo, so he won't take a notion to jump."

"All set," said Dynamo. "I hope you know what we're doing."

JOE PUSHED the button. Two panels slipped inward

and a whoosh of wind sounded.

"Roll in!" Joe shouted. It was a superfluous command. They were rolling, drawn by the rush of wind into the big vacuum capsule. They tumbled together, the panels slid shut, and the capsule darted into motion. The low *whissss* became a barely audible screech as they gathered speed. They slowed for a sharp turn, and Joe knew they had passed the knee joint. Thin bars of blue light illuminated the gliding car. Both Dynamo and Mouse looked like death.

The next whirling curve was taken at high speed. Joe held his breath. This was the zone where the electrocuting rays had worked, out on the surface of the Iron Man's hips. But that danger spot was already passed. The car was rising into the chest.

"We're coming up!" Dynamo cried against the fine screech.

Joe had the same sensation—as though the Iron man were rising.

"We're riding wild," Mouse muttered. "We're going round in circles."

"You're used to air shafts, that's all," Dynamo cracked.

They groped for a solid footing in the rounded end of the capsule and knew they were rising straight up into the iron giant's head. They slowed up and drew to a stop. The door opened and they clambered out dizzily.

They were on a high observation platform within the frame of the Iron Man's head. Thin lines of light illuminated its emptiness. The outer rail offered a view down into the depths of the machinery-filled chest Joe could see dimly the division lines of the great metal units that had come together to form the body.

"Hold up, there, Mouse," Dynamo barked. "We'll all explore this tin soldier together."

Mouse had moved toward the big sphere that occupied the central position within the circular platform. The inner rail surrounding the sphere recessed toward a single oval-shaped door, bright silver within a red metal frame.

"I never figured we'd find this place deserted," Dynamo said. "Shall we try the steel igloo? That must be the brain of the works."

They first made two rounds of the circular platform, pistols ready for trouble. They saw not a sign of a human being. The only sounds were the low, smooth hums of power units somewhere down in the vast steel chest.

"We're standing up, all right," Joe said, "There's the city below us."

Open-air slits in the circular walls gave brief glimpses of the dawn-lit world below them. Mouse was staring, as much surprised as anyone by the unsatisfactory view the narrow windows afforded.

"You can't see enough from here to take aim at anything," Joe said. "There's got to be a better vision than this somewhere."

"It must be in that igloo brain," Dynamo said, "or else this devilish thing is being operated from the outside."

"Here's where we go in." Joe turned to Mouse, who was keeping a sullen face and a silent tongue. "Step ahead, Big Shot. Here's where you earn your passage."

Joe motioned toward the silver door in the red frame. He put a pistol to Mouse's back.

"Open it real quiet-like and peek in. If you don't get your everlasting at first glance, move on in and we'll follow. And Dynamo—check the door as it opens. Make sure it doesn't close on us."

"I'll give it a steel block." Dynamo reached into his coat. "What about the explosives?"

"Wait till we see what's in the sphere."

"Okay, lead the way."

MOUSE HESITATED. Joe prompted him with the pistol. Mouse's quivering hand reached out to the latch. At his touch the door swung open silently. Mouse glanced back.

Joe motioned him to go on. Dynamo bent quietly to fasten a solid block in the door. Single file the three of them tiptoed into the big empty ball of white light.

It seemed empty, it was so large, and it contained so little. The lightness of it burned Joe's eyes at first. He tried to look all directions at once. The staff of Venus killers he had expected to find was not here.

"The Iron Man is moving," Dynamo whispered. "There's some kind of window across the way—or is it a screen?"

It was an odd sort of mirror. It must have been fed by lenses all around the giant's head. It had the curve of half a sphere, and it condensed the cyclorama, with hardly any distortion, bringing in the view from all directions at once. Looking across into it, Joe saw the sky, the rising sun, and the wide stretch of land and ocean. It afforded a downward view of the towering form itself.

"No wonder the old boy can spot his enemies from all directions," Dynamo said. "With this gadget he could see a fly on his big toe and a spider web on the moon at the same time. Is he moving?"

"Sure is," Joe muttered. "Hope we don't go on a rampage."

The spherical room in which they stood was hung to maintain its upright position, no matter how the Iron Man might bend about. He was now bending forward. Joe saw the blaze of the spotlight come to a focus on a line of railway tracks a little distance in from the shore—the first thing he himself had looked at.

A surge of dread filled Joe as he watched. He had the horrible premonition that the monster was about to reach down and tear up the tracks. At the same time Joe saw the faint smile on the lips of Mouse Moberly. "Mouse hopes it will happen," Joe thought. "Mouse would like to see this beast of steel tear up a hundred cities so the Venus invaders could pour in."

The steel monster reached a hand down toward the

tracks. Then, to Joe's consternation, the arm drew back. The monster took his headlight off the rail line and straightened up.

"He's stopped," Dynamo said. "He's not going to do it after all."

"Did you touch anything, Dynamo?"

"No, I'm standing right here by you."

"Did you—"

Mouse shook his head.

"Something governed that action," Joe said. "If we can find out what, we'll know how to control this deadly heap of iron."

"It's automatic," said Mouse with a cold metallic voice.

"Well, listen to who's talking," said Dynamo. "Maybe you want to tell us all about it."

"Anyone can see," Mouse said. "We got into the elevator and it went up. Automatic. Winkler and Craddle took the wrong route and ran into an electric fence. Automatic."

"But that's only part of the story," Joe said. "It's like a man. The heart beats. Automatic. The skin breathes. Automatic. But the eyes look down on something that could be destroyed, and what decides? What? Tell me that."

"Automatic," said Mouse.

"Automatic, hell. A minute ago we started to tear up a railroad track. I was scared it would happen. You, Mouse, you wanted it to happen. I saw it in your eye. But how did the darn thing decide?" Joe's eyes swept the rounded ceiling of light. "Is there something in these walls that picks up our thoughts and translates them into action?"

"I think you've hit it right there," Dynamo said.

"We're getting darn close."

Mouse scoffed. "For the last twenty-four hours it has been making what you call decisions, one after another. If all those actions were the reflections of some man's wish, where's the man? Here we find an empty room. Whose thoughts are here to be picked up? There's no one here."

"I'm not so sure," Joe said, "There's something over this way we haven't seen."

"There's room for a man," Dynamo said. "There's all the conveniences of a prison cell." He began poking around among the chests of drawers built into one side of the wall. "There's concentrated food supplies here for a year. There's a water supply, there's a bath—"

"And a small bed," Joe said, "and someone on it."

Back of the electric window, previously obscured from their view, was the cot where the one lone occupant of the Iron Man's head lay, apparently asleep.

"Stir him out of it," Dynamo said.

Joe didn't move. He stared, standing frozen over the pale, glassy-eyed man who looked up at him.

"That must be the devil that's doing all the dirty work," Dynamo said. "Stir him out of it."

Joe reached down and put his hand on the man's wrist. "Ruppert," he said, "What are you doing here?"

CHAPTER TEN

IT WAS A day to be long remembered. For some it was the last day of life on this earth. Fear turned to panic. Terror spread around the globe like wildfire. Each hour of the day new alarms sounded across the continents and over the oceans.

Two new iron men appeared. Great warlike flying ships from the planet Venus were on their way. Seventeen were seen moving in squadron formation around the earth. The sky station six hours out from the earth was captured. Several nearer points were considered expendable. The Lazy Meteor was evacuated.

Newscasters worked like heroes to bring the earth a graphic account of what was happening. Planes and space ships buzzed and whirred and screamed through the skies. Television cameras loaded the air with spectacular scenes from all directions.

In their underground refuges: millions of people watched, horrified. Women as well as children cried and screamed whenever the television screen brought in pictures of the great iron killers, the deadly Iron Men of Venus.

Iron Man Number One waited in the harbor, poised to deliver a death stroke to any ship or building or railway that might take his fancy.

Iron Man Number Two, who appeared in the screen as identical with Number One, was stalking down the coast like a hungry beast. He was showing one of the same whims as Number One: he preferred public buildings. He might have been looking for the capitols of earth governments. With great handfuls of debris from towers he had crushed, he attacked any court or court house or provincial capitol building. He walked inland and ripped up the public parks with his mighty iron feet.

Iron Man Number Three showed a curious preference for airports and spaceports. He walked over the city, unmindful of the rows of apartment houses he was crushing with every step. When he looked down upon the new, modern port where many interplanetary lines had their headquarters, he appeared to go into a rage.

"That is Iron Man Number Three you are watching," the voice explained over television. "He has just demolished the new ten-million-dollar station of the All-Mars Tours."

Watchers who had the fortitude to take in the gruesome sights saw him killing the people who streamed out from the spaceport buildings.

"He's the fiercest of the three," the newscaster declared. "He spares no fence or wire or signal."

THEN THE picture would color up with yellow dust as Number Three went into a rage of kicking. Walls toppled. Fires broke out. Red flames and black clouds of billowing smoke were everywhere.

"There, he's stopped," the announcer said suddenly. "The big guns were trying for him. Maybe they got him. Just a moment, I'll have an official report for you. No, he has stopped, mysteriously. He has not been struck. It must be that some signal stopped him. Perhaps there is an unseen general directing these Iron Men. However, we may have more a little later. As you know, Iron Man Number One has been entered by our forces. The three men who entered are being quizzed at the present moment."

The announcer paused, as if viewing the picture of the boiling smoke.

"I give you my own theory for what it may be worth," the announcer continued. "I believe they are like gigantic tin soldiers, wound up to go a certain length of time. When they run down they stop."

Another newscaster cut in. "The theory you have just heard is not official. However, in support of this view I offer you these two evidences."

Here the screen flashed on a shot of Iron Man Number One, bent toward a railway, but definitely stopped in action. Then came the picture of Iron Man Number Three, standing tall and forbidding amid the fury of flame and smoke, but making no motion.

"Are these Iron men through? Have they shot their wad? Is their show over? Let us hope, but even so, this may be only a preliminary flurry of terrorizing, to precede the real attack by ships."

And so it went, through the underground houses and apartment buildings and storm cellars—wherever people had gathered to wait in fear.

Somewhere twenty-five floors under the surface, Claire Maddergall waited, eyes closed. Her husband was away, taking part in the investigations. Little Penny kept besieging her with questions and protests.

"But Mama, do we have to stay down here? Can't we go where Papa is? If the first Iron Man isn't killing anymore, can't we go up and drive out in the car and see him?"

"No, child, don't even think of such a thing."

"Then he's still dangerous, isn't he. Mama?"

"We don't know dear."

"I wish we could go out and see him. If we'd drive by real fast he couldn't do anything to us, could he, Mama? Could he?"

"We don't know. Penny. Please don't think about it."

"He wouldn't want to kill you, Mama, if he knew how nice you are. He might kill some other folks, but not you."

"Being nice doesn't seem to make any difference."

"He might kill Papa, mightn't he?"

"Why, Penny?"

"I mean if he kills everybody—"

"Yes, dear" Claire slipped her arm around the child's body and wondered whether her little thoughts had found room for some suspicion of Paul Maddergall. How much might a little child know? And how much was there to know about Paul, his secret dealings with Zuber and Mouse Moberly and the Venus Storm Colony? Claire trembled to ask herself such questions.

But she did ask them over and over as her suspicions of her husband grew. How simple it would be, she thought suddenly, for her and little Penny to get into their new red sports car and spin straight down the avenue toward the Iron Man. Yes, within reach of it.

And if it should strike—

If it did, she and her child would never know the depth of her husband's guilt, of how vast his traitorous actions.

"Penny," Claire said suddenly, "would you like very much to take a ride in our new red car—"

"To look at the Iron Man?"

"Yes, dear."

"Oh, Mama, could we?"

SOMEWHERE in the mountains, many miles from the

scenes of destruction, an aged man and his daughter watched the little television screen. Every hour they breathed their quiet thanks to the young man who had been so kind to them. They might have been left in the path of ruin, as helpless as babes. But Joe Kane had happened to come their way, and had given them the will and the courage—and the money—to escape.

"Mary," the old man called feebly. "Mary, come and see. It's him again. It's that boy Kane. See at the right of the screen. They're questioning him again."

ELEVATOR service was bad all day in the underground apartment building where Joe Kane lived. The elevator man was too busy running off to the handiest television screens.

"That's him. That's Joe, all right. And there's his pal, Dynamo. They're the guys who climbed into the Iron man to see what makes him work."

"You mean those boys live right here in this building?"

"Eighteen floors down. I haul them back and forth every day."

"Isn't that where we heard the prowlers last night?"

"Yep, Joe and Dynamo catched all three of them—with my help, that is I sprung the trap for 'em, and they did the rest. I could have had my picture in the paper, but me, I'm just naturally modest…looks like I ought to be there helping Joe right now, the way they're firing the questions at him. They're tying him in knots, sounds like…gee whiz, what does that guy mean, trying to accuse Joe?"

CHAPTER ELEVEN

THE NEWSCASTERS had praised Joe and Dynamo only a few minutes before. Very daring chaps. They had found their way into the Iron Man's brain. What they knew might help to turn the tide.

But ironically, the quizzing of important men suddenly

put Joe and Dynamo on the defensive.

"What is your explanation, Mr. Dinkins, about the explosives? Why didn't you plant them in his head and set them off as planned?"

"I—I don't know," Dynamo stammered. "Joe was the boss. I guess we were so dizzy we forgot."

"Dizzy? You were grossly inefficient," Paul Maddergall said. "I don't think you ever intended to obey the command."

"But we were dizzy. It was like on a high building, only higher. And when it moved we could feel ourselves weaving around. You should go up, Mr. Maddergall," Dynamo said frankly. "Mouse Moberly said he was going around in circles."

"Mr. Kane," Maddergall said, taking a sadistic delight in this new chance to make Joe squirm, "it's up to you to answer the questions. You are on the spot, Mr. Kane. Do you understand? "

Joe narrowed his eyes in the direction of the brittle questioner. "I understand, sir, that I didn't accomplish everything. But I've made a start. And what I did was done in good faith."

The other men around the table were made uneasy by Maddergall's tactics, but he meant to play the game his way. He beat his fist upon the table. "Your expedition involved three men who went under protest. Two of them lost their lives. You say you entered the mechanical brain of the Iron Man, and that you believe his actions are the result of this brain's workings—in response to the will of its occupants. You had a chance to set off explosions in the brain, yet you didn't. Are you following me, Mr. Kane?"

"Yes, sir."

"Worst of all," Maddergall pointed an accusing finger in Joe's face, "when you discovered the man who occupied this diabolical brain, what did you do? Did you treat him as an enemy and shoot him on the spot? No. You ran the risk of taking him prisoner. And when you brought him back to us, what did we find? We found that he was your brother. Right?"

"I guess so, sir."

"You guess so…indeed."

"But even if he hadn't been my brother I'd have tried to bring him back here alive—for questioning."

Much to Joe's relief, Commander Doyle nodded his approval. "Yes, you're certainly right on that point. With more Iron Men moving in on us, I consider the most important immediate step in our campaign is to discover the key to these monsters' actions."

Maddergall was quick to put himself on the right side. "Exactly, Commander. I was just coming to that. What I'm asking Mr. Kane is, did he find the key—the trick—the secret—the gadget—whatever you want to call the process by which these steel beasts guide their actions? The obvious answer is, he did not. He was right in the presence of it, and he muffed it."

"But Mr. Maddergall—" Chairman Helva started to protest; but Paul Maddergall would not be stopped.

"He muffed his chance. How do we know but what he failed on purpose? I hereby recommend that he and his brother Ruppert be charged with high treason against the governments of the earth."

JOE SAW that his hands were white as chalk. The sergeant-at-arms was glaring at him, just daring him to try any rough stuff. Yet something made him rise and point squarely at Maddergall. He wanted to say that Maddergall would pay for that false charge. But when he found his voice, quavering with anger, he said nothing of the kind.

"If you really want to find the secret of the Iron Man—why don't you let my brother help? Or is he still alive? "

The eyes of the men around the table turned to Dr.

Kenilworth, a short, keen-eyed young man with a plump face and a thin black mustache. His voice was gentle but strong with authority.

"Ruppert Kane has been too ill for questioning. He has been the victim of severe shock. I don't think that anything he might say at the present time would have the slightest value—however, those in charge are making careful records. If you would like, I'll give you a recording of our conversations."

The committee of inquiry listened eagerly. The voice of Ruppert was like the voice of a mother or a father moved with deep grief over the loss of a child. It was a cry, a heart-rending chant, a sobbing plea for peace...for no more killing...no more destroying. "Please, no! No, no, it mustn't happen."

Maddergall, looking very sour at how things were going, muttered, "Sounds like he got his fill of it. More than be bargained for. But I wouldn't trust him to go back into that iron monster."

"Where is he now?" Commander Doyle asked.

The doctor smiled. "You may think it strange, but I have placed him out in the sunshine on the open plaza at the top of this building."

"Where he can watch the Iron Man?"

"Yes, that's so. I consider that we are at a safe distance. It seems to give him relief and assurance to know that the monster is not moving."

"If he thinks he can win any mercy for himself with a ruse like that—" But Maddergall was cut short.

"Just a moment," Commander Doyle said. "If I may have the floor."

Chairman Helva gratefully recognized the commander. "Go ahead, Doyle. Untangle this if you can."

"Thank you." The commander turned a sharp look on Kane and Dinkins, "These gentlemen, in my opinion, have done a heroic thing—even if they fell short of our hopes in some respects. I think it's only fair that we give them another chance…that is…if they want it."

Everyone looked at Joe, waiting for him to speak. He stared at his hands. Dynamo remained silent.

"What do you say, gentlemen? Do you think you have enough nerve left to have another go at it?"

Joe spoke slowly. "We have the nerve—yes. And if it's your wish…we'll go."

THE ROOM, almost completely silent, echoed the sound of light tottering footsteps entering the open door. Everyone turned at the sound of a broken voice, speaking huskily. In the doorway stood Ruppert Kane, his eyes staring like death, his hand trembling. A hospital attendant supported him as he moved into the room.

"I heard," he said. "I came to say…that you, Joe…you must not enter the Iron Man's head again. Rather than have you go…I would kill you."

That was what be had come to say. He turned around and the hospital attendant led him out.

"That's it," Joe muttered to himself. "I see it now." He came to his feet suddenly, breaking the silence that had taken possession of the room. "I'm not sure, but I may know how to prove—no that wouldn't be possible. It might take days—still—"

"Mr. Kane, are you just talking to yourself?" asked Chairman Helva. "If you are, you're getting nowhere. However, if you can explain a little further and share with us how you think the Iron Men work—and more importantly, how we can defeat them—then I'm in favor of giving you and Mr. Dinkins another chance."

"Chairman, what I want to do won't be easy. But I think it will prove—yes—yes, I think it will work." Joe got an excited look on his face. Dynamo nudged him and Kane did his best to look composed. "In order for me to prove what I have in mind we're going to need to raid those Venus ships and capture a few men. I need three—at least three. And they've got to have pretty strong feelings against us."

"If everyone here agrees, we might be able work it," Commander Doyle said. It's going to take a number of hours, though. Perhaps a day or two."

"No…no…now that I think about it, we probably don't need to wait for hours or days. I think we can do it now—right now."

"What are you talking about?" Maddergall demanded.

Joe looked slowly in Maddergall's direction. "I'm thinking of you, Mr. Maddergall—sir." Joe looked at the other officials in the room and thumbed toward Maddergall. "He's the one that can help us prove it. With his help, we can prove it right away."

They all stared at Kane, and they were all speechless. But Commander Doyle must have recognized the spark in his eyes. He seemed to know it meant that Joe Kane knew what he was talking about. Doyle, standing tall and tense, said, "Gentlemen, I don't know exactly what Mr. Kane is trying to prove, but I think we might give him some leeway. Our country and—yes—even our world are in desperate straits—and I'm in favor of letting him have his way, at least to a certain point. Is there anyone here who objects?"

"He's saying that this would somehow involve me?" Maddergall asked.

"You." Joe said, almost smiling. "Yes, Paul…you'd be the first one to help put the theory to a test." Joe waved his finger at Maddergall and shook his head. "And if you want to help solve our trouble you *can't…say…no.*"

There was a long silence. Maddergall started to turn red. Then Joe said, "Are you with us, Paul?"

Maddergall got up storming. "Who the devil is this man to question my loyalty?"

"Quiet, Paul," Helva said calmly, rapping on the table. "I believe we're all in agreement to give these two men another chance. Now if they feel that you can help then out…" The Chairman gave Maddergall a long hard look. "…then I think you should do everything you can for them. Are you with us on this?"

"Not at the price of my life."

"Even if it saves the lives of millions?"

Maddergall looked away and sat down. A moment later he gave out a long sigh. "All right…let's hear the scheme. What is it?"

"Just this," Joe said. "You make the trip up into the Iron Man's head. You enter the brain alone. You stay for an hour. Then you come back down. That's it."

"You mean I go alone?"

"Take a bodyguard if you wish, to make sure you get back safely—just so you and you alone go inside the brain."

"What if the thing starts acting up while I'm inside?"

Commander Doyle spoke up, "If that happens, Paul, you should do everything you can to ascertain why it's becoming active again." Then he looked over at Joe. "But I do have one other question for you. Is there any reason why Maddergall should go instead of someone else?"

Joe was thoughtful with his answer. "Every reason. I'd like you to give me that leeway you mentioned a minute ago, Doyle." He looked back toward Maddergall. "As long as Paul—and only Paul—enters the brain, I'm pretty sure that the iron man will reek no further destruction."

Ten minutes later, Paul Maddergall and a party of handpicked guards set out for the ankle entrance to the Iron Man.

CHAPTER TWELVE

WITHIN A few minutes after Maddergall and his bodyguard had left, Commander Doyle approached Joe and said, "Would you mind telling me this brainstorm of yours?"

"You're the one I trust," Joe said. "I'll tell it all to you—

and anyone who will believe me. You see, Dynamo and I have been barnstorming around mostly by trial and error, but at the same time—hey, what happened to Dynamo?"

"He left," the commander said. "He asked my permission. I'm trusting him the same as I would you."

Joe looked about in a state of worry. "I hope he didn't get a notion to go up into one of those Iron Men again."

"The fact is, that's where he's going. He heard that Iron Man Number Three had stopped moving, and he said he thought he could find his way in."

"But he mustn't," Joe said excitedly. "Can we stop him? If not that iron man will tear up the earth."

Doyle put a calming hand on Joe's shoulder. "He said you'd be worried. He said to tell you he was taking Mouse Moberly for a mascot and that Mouse would be with him every minute."

Joe stared for a moment with a blank expression, then began to smile. "Say, maybe Dynamo knows what the score is too. He'll have Mouse with him every minute? Well...yes, it might be all right."

They ascended to the plaza on the surface. Dr. Kenilworth, who had been talking with Ruppert, making certain his patient was comfortable, came over to join Joe and the commander.

"Joe," Commander Doyle said, "is about to give us his explanation of the Iron Men's antics, but first he wanted to ask you about the experiments on brain waves, electrical accompaniments to emotional slates and the like. Are you familiar with this field, doctor?"

"Yes, I am," Kenliworth said, "but unfortunately, the greatest experimenter, and I should say the greatest authority in this field, was cut short in his career here on Earth. This happened several years ago. I won't go into a lot of detail, but he was involved in some pretty serious criminal activities and was deported to a penal colony on Venus."

"Then it's possible," Joe said, "that these Venus killers

might have made new advances in this particular area of scientific research?"

"If this man fell into their hands then it's certainly possible—perhaps even likely—that they have outdistanced us. Do you think this area of science is somehow involved in the operational basis of the electronic brains that control these creatures? Do you think that human brain waves are somehow necessary for their operation?"

"Yes—that is—in a twisted sort of way."

"Meaning what?"

"This may sound a little crazy to you at first, Doctor, but don't judge me too quickly...please," Joe said earnestly. He paused for a moment, looking off into the distance as though contemplating the exact words he needed. He then leaned in close to the doctor's face and in a low, but firm voice said, "I believe it's possible that whatever one is feeling...whatever one is wishing for...while inside an iron man's brain and near its receptors...is basically executed by the iron men—*in reverse.*"

Doyle and Kenilworth didn't say anything for a minute. The three men walked along the railing of the plaza, looking across the harbor to the tall figure of Iron Man Number One, towering into the low summer clouds. He was bent a trifle, as if intending to make wreckage of the railway yards beneath him.

"For example?" asked Commander Doyle.

"For example, the way Number One has struck down everything and everyone that my brother Ruppert would not want injured. Ruppert probably awoke to find himself in an Iron Monster that was walking through the ocean, powered by some automatic mechanism. Now I know my brother, and the first thing that would occur to Ruppert would be the danger of striking a boat. His frenzied fear that a boat might be hit would have been received by receptors within the electric brain around him—interpreted electronically—then reversed. In other words, a wish to preserve life would be changed into a wish to destroy life. And the Iron Man's mechanism would go into action fulfilling the reversed brain waves."

"Yes, go on."

"My brother Ruppert would look down in terror and see a few survivors. He would wish them safety. Then the steel monstrosity would have picked them up and one by one, and subjected them to a horrible death."

"I recall," said the doctor, "that the Iron Man made wreckage of the Interplanetary Museum."

"One of my brother's favorite haunts."

"On the other hand it passed over the well known gambling house—"

"Which was perhaps the one place in the city that Ruppert would wish destroyed...as long as be saw the destruction going on, he was too concerned to turn away from the view; and the more he watched, the more his sympathies were aroused—which, in turn, prompted more destruction."

"H-m-m. I wonder." Commander Doyle puzzled. "I wonder why the Venus killers should have chosen to set it up in that reversed arrangement. Why not occupy the Iron Men themselves, and let their own destructive wishes be carried out directly?"

"Possibly they wanted to dodge their own guilt as long as possible."

"Yes, but more important, they don't trust each other," Joe said. "They seem to cooperate, all right, when they're coming to attack us. But from what Ruppert has told me I know that they hate each other. If they had occupied the Iron Men themselves, their real wishes would have been felt and they would have been at each other's throats. It was safer for them to put the whole business in reverse, and let innocent people like Ruppert be their tools."

THE COMMANDER interrupted. "Look, the Iron Man

is beginning to move. That means that Maddergall has now entered the brain. The monster is coming to life again."

"If the destruction begins all over," the doctor said, "he'll surely have the wits to come out."

"He was supposed to stay an hour," Joe said.

"An hour's destruction is a high price to pay for the proof we wanted."

"But I'm convinced there'll be no destruction," Joe said. "That's why I insisted on Maddergall."

"You mean—"

"I happen to know he'd like a path of death and ruin to make way for his Venus friends. No matter what he's saying to himself this minute as he stands in the Iron Man's brain, the wish is there, burning in his heart and his mind. The monster will give us that wish in reverse. It will refuse to destroy."

Commander Doyle held binoculars to his eyes, taking in the massive head that peered down through the thin clouds. Sometimes the spotlight, brightly ablaze through the afternoon light, played across the waters toward the plaza. At other times it illuminated the lines of traffic moving at what was considered a safe distance.

The doctor was regarding Joe with interest. "If what you believe is true, Kane, how does it happen that no great destruction took place while you were up in the Iron Man's head? I should think your love for our ships and harbors and buildings and parks would have resulted in some hard pounding of those iron fists."

Joe smiled. "I played in luck. I happened to have someone with me who came under protest—Mouse Moberly, Old man Zuber's top executive. That little hard-willed devil walked into the brain at the same time I did, with a pistol at his back. Whatever Dynamo and I may have wished while we were in there, Mouse's traitorous wishes counteracted us. But this I remember distinctly. We had gotten Ruppert out onto the platform and were about the take the elevator down when I decided to go back for a final look. For a moment Mouse wasn't there to counterbalance me. In that moment the Iron Man reached down and tore up a big railway station and half a mile of track. And in that minute or two I knew what an awful thing Ruppert had gone through. There couldn't be a more frustrating experience. You look down at one person; you scream, hoping he'll get out of the way—and the steel hand instantly kills him. When that happens four or five times, you begin to get the feeling that you're doing it. Every good wish makes you all the more guilty. In a little while you'd go mad."

The doctor nodded. He looked across to Ruppert. "I can begin to understand what that poor fellow has been through."

"He was completely down when we found him."

"Exhaustion. A sort of spiritual exhaustion." The doctor brightened. "I believe, though, that he has the constitution to come out of it."

Alarms were sounding. The iron monster had begun to take great strides across the harbor. It was in fact moving in the general direction of the plaza where the commander, Joe and the doctor were standing.

"We'd better go down under," the doctor said. "We'll have to move the patient down. I don't want any nervous relapses."

Ruppert was shaking his head. He was asking the attendant to let him stay. Commander Doyle was standing his ground, too, as if the sirens hadn't penetrated his ears. He was watching intently through the binoculars. Suddenly he said, "Joe, what happens if Maddergall sees something he likes very much—something he loves?"

"The Iron Man would destroy it. Whatever Maddergall's emotional drift is, the monster will play it in reverse." Joe paused. "Why are you asking? What do you see?"

"There's something red in the Iron Man's hand. He picked it up out of the traffic just before he started over this way. It's an automobile...and I think there's a lady and a child in it."

CHAPTER THIRTEEN

"STAND CLOSE by me," Ruppert said to the others in his weak voice. He was watching the Iron Man move across the harbor toward them.

"Are you afraid?" the doctor asked.

"Not for myself. For you. I'm in no danger. You see, Maddergall hates me like poison…so the iron hands won't touch me."

Joe patted Ruppert on the shoulder. Clear thoughts were coming back to that tortured mind. It was plain that Ruppert had discovered for himself the awful relationship between wish and action within the monster's complex makeup.

"It's coming closer. It's shining its light on us. What's going to happen?" The doctor stood courageously, almost defiantly. The dark steel form came towering over them. In its hand it held the red sports roadster—held it cunningly, so that the two occupants being carried high above the water sat in safety.

The headlight blazed down, making the plaza look like a stage. It was a strange drama that took place there. Only those who understood the reverse of motives could appreciate what was happening. The Iron Man worked rapidly and precisely, as if knowing exactly what be wanted to do. The huge fingers set the car down within a few feet of Ruppert. In a steel grasp that couldn't have been entirely tender, the fingers lifted Claire from the car and placed her beside Ruppert. With a definite motion of persuasion, it pushed the two of them toward each other.

"The very thing that Maddergall wants least in the world—for them to come back together," Commander Doyle murmured, nodding toward Joe.

Joe, however, was foreseeing something that looked very much like murder. Little Penny had been left sitting in the car. Like her mother, she was speechless from awe and terror. Claire Maddergall cried toward her, then fell into a faint. The doctor and Ruppert drew her back into the shelter of an alcove, and Joe only hoped they would find their way down out of sight before the Iron Man committed his next inevitable deed.

Now the big hand swept roughly at the car that contained the six-year old child. It skidded sidewise across the plaza. It bumped against the railing and for an instant the hand paused. Joe was on the run, and the split second of hesitation gave him his chance. He leaped for the car, caught the side, clung like a bulldog. The child was screaming.

The rail was knocked out as if made of toothpicks. The car was swept over into the harbor. Joe went down with it. Metal was crunching around him. He rolled frantically and wrapped the child in his arms. He plunged out as the car swooshed down into the water.

He dived deep. The child might drown in his arms. That would be better than allowing it to be crushed in the grip of steel.

He struggled to swim under water. The child's fingers dug into his flesh. Strangely he was thinking of Maddergall. Up in that twisted brain Maddergall must be watching it all happen, unable to take his eyes from the horror of it, screaming inwardly against the tragedy of it. If so, his love for his child only hastened the Iron Man's deadly strokes. Through the water came the sounds of crunching metal once again. Then a *whoosh* of water told Joe that the monster hand had lifted and gone.

The low concussions of giant footsteps sounded. The Iron Man walked a few steps and came to a stop. Perhaps Maddergall had emerged from the brain by this time.

Joe came to the surface gasping for air. The drowned child in his arms was a sad sight. He moved along the path at the shore line, uncertain which way to go. Then he saw the doctor and Commander Doyle rushing down to him. The doctor took the child. There was always a chance, if they worked fast and carefully...

THE ATTACK of seventeen warships out of space began at sundown. The whole armada came on before midnight. The earth's defenses met them head on. For three days the attack continued with fierce intensity. Then the surviving Venus killers limped back across the skies, soundly defeated.

The earth had withstood the test. Though several major cities had suffered severe blows, the invaders campaign failed to come off as planned. It was stymied by surprise actions on the part of the Iron Men. These monsters of Venus steel had miraculously turned against their builders and gone to the side of the defenders. A simple switch had turned the trick. Locked within their brains were the three men who hoped passionately to profit from a Venus victory—Moberly, Zuber and Maddergall.

These three, the best of friends in their world of schemes, were perfect for their job. As the Venus warships flew in over the Iron Men in their carefully planned routine, blazing pistols from the monsters' guns sliced them from stem to stern. They fell in heaps with their loads of bombs and men.

The earth could only guess how its three traitors felt to bring such a defeat upon themselves. The men locked in the brains must have been inspired to march up onto the continents and destroy everything with their own iron hands. They must have—for their wish was reversed by the giants of steel. Disobedient as always, the Iron Men moved out to sea. There, it was related by scouting planes, Moberly and Zuber recognized each other, and would gladly have joined forces. But their deep friendship now boomeranged. The two Iron Men fought each other with the ferocity of war to the death, and went down into the sea fighting.

Maddergall, it was believed, wanted nothing more than to go back to his wife, to possess her, and to make amends, if possible, for murdering his own daughter. Instead, the stubborn monster took him deeper and deeper into the ocean. It was said to have come to rest a hundred feet below the surface somewhere out in the Atlantic. "He has food and water for a year," came the report of the earth governments. "He will not be disturbed."

Many softhearted people, however, felt that he should have been informed, somehow, that his six-year old daughter had escaped the fate of the Iron Man's death grip. She had been rescued almost miraculously by Joe Kane; the water had been expelled from her lungs and life breathed into her by the swift actions of Dr. Kenilworth. Her mother, Clair, had found Ruppert again, and would no longer bear the name of Maddergall.

JOE HAD wondered all along about the earthmen who had been forced into the Iron Men's brains, and who—besides Ruppert—had undergone this ordeal. He was not surprised to learn that Iron Man Number Two had contained a highly patriotic citizen whose murder had been cunningly faked to mask his disappearance. Senator Droondair, thought murdered, had actually been snatched by killer spies to be used in one of the monster brain compartments.

As to the occupant of Iron Man Number Three, Joe was left in the dark during the thick of the battle. He was a pretty busy man during those tense hours. He had been made a special aide to Commander Doyle. Dynamo, in turn, served as his bodyguard. Refusing a uniform, Dynamo stuck to his tattered coat with the many pockets, which afforded Venus knives or ice-cooled grape pop as needed.

When the smoke of battle thinned, Joe was pleased to learn that a girl named Mary had sent him a message of appreciation, saying, "I think you are wonderful, Joe, and I hope I see you again some day." Joe smiled.

"Do you figure to see her again?" Dynamo asked, somewhat at a loss to explain the wistful behavior of his best friend.

"It might happen that way," Joe said with a far-away look.

But one quite sad note had to be added to the conclusion of the brief war. It came to Joe in the form of a letter—two letters—and a coat.

"Been meaning to give you these," Dynamo said. "I picked them up the day Mouse and I rode up into Iron Man Number Three."

Number Three, Joe recalled, had all but obliterated the best spaceports and then had mysteriously stopped, frozen into immobility in the act of destroying.

"It was Lanny we found in Number Three," Dynamo said, "We found him there dead. You wouldn't have wanted to see him. You won't see him now because his body was lost in the first wave of attacks—"

"Lanny? My brother Lanny?"

"You thought he was dead before. Maybe I shouldn't have told you otherwise. But I figure, from the way I found him in the brain of Number Three, that he took his own life to stop the killing of others. He had gotten a hold of your coat, somehow, and these two letters were in the pocket."

JOE SKIMMED through the first letter. It was the message that had been handed to him during that first bad hour on the witness stand. He had pocketed it, but never had a chance to open it.

It was Lanny's handwriting, scrawled in great haste. "...I'm sure they'll knock out my ship to screen this kidnapping. They're going to use me for their attack somehow. I'm helpless...we're pausing at a space station. Just a break that I may get a chance to send this...to let you know I've been kidnapped..."

The second letter had been written while Lanny was a prisoner within the brain of Number Three.

"...I can't understand, Joe, how your coat happened to fly into this place. Don't you open your mail? Maybe they've got you, too..."

And the letter went on to describe Lanny's being forced into one of the parts of the Iron Man before it slid into the sea; and how later he thought he had found an escape into daylight, only to discover that he was now trapped within a ball of light, where the view came to him.

At the last, he was agonized and helpless. Somehow his will was being twisted into destruction. Every prayer he breathed increased the vigor of the monster. He could not go on spreading death and ruin. "For the sake of those innocent I'm looking down upon, for the sake of the country I love, I must end it…"

"Lanny was a good boy," Dynamo said. "We're going to miss him."

"He was a swell kid; one of my favorite brothers," Joe said.

THE END

SCIENCE AT THE CROSSROADS IN A NEW UNIVERSE

The Universe had grown so vast that time and space had taken on new meanings for mankind—especially for those engaged in the world of science. Man's millenium-long progress toward the stars and beyond had forever changed the destiny of Earth. Yet in spite of all his progress, man could still be a bit of a brute at times, so planetary conflicts, even galactic war, still remained a looming possibility. Yes…human nature was still as fiery and unpredictable as ever. How then, could one extraordinarily unusual man make sanity prevail?

"The Man with Absolute Motion" is a forgotten science fiction gem, filled with intrigue and thought-provoking situations, penned by veteran author Noel Loomis.

CAST OF CHARACTERS

ERLE BERTRON

One of the only "normal" humans on the face of the Earth. Was he a sideshow freak, or the savior of the Universe?

NAOMI

She was the first "normal" woman Bertron had ever met—and he fell head over heals in love with her.

VOLMIK

This evil galactic ruler had notions of controlling all of the energy sources throughout the entire cosmos.

YJUL

He was a genius who knew more about energy than anyone in the universe—even if he was just a plant.

GENERAL REMIGGON

The most powerful governmental official in the metagalaxy, and his entire being was contained in a small, floating purple ball!

ADMIRAL BLOMBERG

He was the bitter, frustrated representative of a dying planet. Unfortunately, that planet happened to be Earth.

MARISSA

She was the Admiral's wife, but her affections for another man threatened the safety of the cosmos.

EKNO

This veteran space pilot hoped to become the first creature to pilot a ship powered by absolute motion.

THE MAN WITH ABSOLUTE MOTION

By
NOEL LOOMIS

ARMCHAIR FICTION & MUSIC
PO Box 4369, Medford, Oregon 97504

For more information about Armchair Books and products, visit our website at…

www.armchairfiction.com

Or email us at…

armchairfiction@yahoo.com

"I dinna believe that this is the only warl' Gweed made. I'm sure there wis some connached [spoiled] in the makin', an' there's maybe a place at the back o' the Univairse faur there is bits o' warl's half made, lumps o' airth an' so on. A' sweepit awa' tae Infeenity wi' the Besom o' Destruction," —Alex Macgregor, Aberdeen, Scotland. Reprinted by permission of THE COUNTRYMAN, *Burford, OxfordsPire, England.*

CHAPTER ONE

ADMIRAL BLOMBERG, United Earth Space Service, called from the bathroom, "Will you take my white dress uniform from the fresh-up cabinet, dear?"

His wife, a lovely, cream-skinned brunette with a platinum stripe down the middle of her hair, and tawny golden-flecked eyes—they were heavy-lidded like the eyes of a lazy cat—didn't stir from the chaise lounge. "I forgot to put it in there," she said.

Marissa was a first thirty-six, while the admiral, a hundred and forty-two and on his second Osterhus, was short and round-faced and a little bald. His eyes were a mild blue. He said, "Put it there," and Marissa got up to obey.

Marrisa wasn't happy stuck away on Regulus, among the representatives of peoples of half a trillion planets, but she could still obey. He did wish she wouldn't use that particular shade of violet on her fingernails, but he didn't want to make an issue of it.

"It isn't often an Earth-person is even allowed to enter Regulus City," he pointed out.

She studied him, and he knew she was bored and hoping to stir up some excitement. "The greatest city in all the Second Metagalaxy," she said, "built on a burning star, with foundations sunken in a bed of stripped nuclei"—she paused for effect, making it obvious that she was parroting what he

Man's millennium-long progress
toward the stars had changed the face
of the Earth and warped his human heritage.
But there was sanity — a fiery sword in darkness.

had first told her— "with blue-green flames enveloping us a hundred thousand miles over our heads." She yawned.

"Wonderful engineering, dear, but *so* dull after you've seen it."

He wished Marissa would pick her days better, but then Marissa had her own ideals, and he well knew that she never failed to pick an important day to stir things up. If he didn't tell her the day would be important, she seemed to sense it somehow.

Some time later he sat in a complex of magnetic currents in the office of Space General Remiggon, secretary for the Metagalactic Conference. The room was large and its ornamentation was on the quiet side, with waving bands of pastel light that followed, one another from the floor, progressively deepening in color, until they faded into a black ceiling with twinkling red, yellow, orange, blue, green, and white pinpoints arranged like the Milky Way—the Second Metagalaxy, to be technical—seen from the south celestial pole. Metagalactic pole again, he reminded himself, for the orientation was not from the position of Earth.

The door dropped softly behind him, and Blomberg glanced again at the desk. There was about it something odd even for this part of the universe. It was an opaque purple ball, apparently seamless and evenly colored, hanging suspended in the atmosphere two feet above the desk—at about the level of Blomberg's face.

It had no visible connection with anything else in the room, except that on top there was a tiny aerial that resembled the microwave aerials commonly found on large spaceships. But though the device was just as complicated, with hundreds of wires and planes and parabaloid disks, it hardly equaled in height the length of Blomberg's hand.

A voice came from a transmuter somewhere. "Sit down, admiral, and help yourself to a cigar. They're from Havana, you know," A chuckle. "It's odd, isn't it, that no other sentient species in the Fourth Universe has taken up your

Earth habit of smoking."

Blomberg had been in space long enough not to be disturbed because he was unable to locate the source of the voice. You got used to a lot of strange things when you patrolled the vast inter-spacial areas of the Pass at the speed of light in a ship big enough to house a large city. And even stranger things when you penetrated the great clouds of ionized iron and calcium to explore the abysmal Deeps in ships that traveled at the compounded square of the speed of light. So he casually sat down and lit the cigar, taking in the full mellowness of its aroma.

The purple ball gently came to rest on top of the desk, and Blomberg continued to watch it sharply above his cigar.

"We Regulians are one of the few non-humanoid sentient forms in the Fourth Universe," the voice said. "We're a rather weird life form from your point of view, but I hope you won't mind. We were highly civilized, and possessed clairvoyance, telekinesis, and teleportation when that damned star came along and threw our planet into a tizzy."

The voice paused an instant, then went on quickly, "We decided then and there we'd take no more risks like that. Some of the older heads were born millions of years ago, you know, and the knowledge that you are immortal inclines one to caution. We—well, we appointed a committee to work out plans for adapting ourselves to live on Rigel. It's a big star and quite hot, as you know; But that offered no great problem. To sum it up, we've been here ever since. The mass of the thing is our protection, of course."

"I would think," Blomberg said, digesting all this carefully, "that it would have been a little hard to get used to living on a ball of incandescent gas."

"A little difficult at first," the voice conceded, "But we all like it now. In fact, I get violently homesick when I am on my periodical inspection trips."

Blomberg tapped his cigar, scowling at the purple ball, "One can get accustomed to almost anything," he murmured, and was surprised to see the cigar ash go upward instead of falling to the floor. He followed it with his eyes until it disappeared in the ceiling.

"Especially treated to resist gravitation," the voice informed him. "Well, I'm General Remiggon."

Blomberg was scrutinizing the ball, trying to decide where to look when he addressed the general. Certainly there was nothing that remotely resembled eyes.

"Just look at my middle," the general suggested.

"Thank you, sir," Blomberg said, experiencing a slight feeling of dizziness.

"I can see no reason," said the general, "why we should not dispense with formalities."

Blomberg looked at him incredulously, "As space general of the line, sir, with a ten-thousand-year record of action behind you, you outrank me considerably."

"Unimportant," said Remiggon. "As one of Earth's ranking officers, you are working for Earth, aren't you?"

"Yes," Blomberg conceded. "For Earth primarily."

The general nodded. "And I am working for the metagalaxy. Call me Remiggon. Now, Blomberg, I'm glad that you have your speech well in mind."

"My speech? Well, you see—"

"You were about to say that a while ago you were worrying more about your wife than you were about your mission."

"That was—er—temporary, I assure you."

"You'd really save yourself a lot of trouble by eliminating the two sexes on Earth," Remiggon observed.

"Yes. We'd also eliminate a basic interest."

The purple ball was silent for an instant. "Proceed."

"Sir, Earth and its population face a dilemma in which the

very existence of the human race is at stake." Blomberg paused impressively.

"I know your speech," the general said. "I can recite it backward. Let's get on with the discussion."

Blomberg hesitated, "I find it disconcerting, sir, to find my very thoughts jerked, so to speak, out of my brain."

A chuckle came from the purple ball. "I assume you have had this problem sent up to our Technical Department."

"Yes, sir—and they told us it would take sixteen hundred years to get a decision even with rush emergency."

"You appealed on the basis of the welfare of the species, didn't you?"

Blomberg studied his cigar. "Sir, if you will forgive me, I know our Earth government is clumsy, but—"

Remiggon sounded a little impatient. "Let me tell you, young man—don't stare at me; I'll never see a hundred thousand again—the metagalaxy is vast, and—"

"I know, sir, but—"

"If you refuse to listen," said Remiggon, "I'll sit you on a stool wearing a dance cup."

"The words are dunce cap," said Blomberg.

"Sorry. That confounded smoke muddles up your mind. Your question is on genetics and it is not simple. If it were, I would answer it myself. The only warranted basis for a faster answer would be galactic necessity—and you can't claim that."

"It's vital to us."

"But not to the galaxy. My dear admiral, you've probably forgotten your cosmological geography."

"Probably, sir."

"The Fourth Universe contains eight decimal point times ten to the twenty-seventh cubic parsecs," Remiggon said impressively. "Get that? Those are parsecs, not your puny miles."

"A parsec is twenty trillion miles," Blomberg said slowly.

Remiggon nodded. "The Cosmos is, incredibly more vast. For instance, not even the Universe Dioclave knows what universe adjoins us below Achernar. So you can see that anything remotely resembling a government of the metagalaxy must of necessity be loose."

"It could get cumbersome," Blomberg admitted.

"Let me do a little elementary arithmetic. In the first place, the Second Metagalaxy averages ten decimal point one inhabited planets per star. That means four hundred billion planets. Most of these, like your Earth, are in a somewhat primitive stage, for the Fourth is a comparatively young universe. Now suppose that from all the sentient species on an inhabited planet, one question is allowed per year—or *all* species, understand, not for each. That's four hundred billion requests per year. Now, take one request. Assume that an expert in Technical can work out all the angles and provide an answer in ten days.

"Actually, I say again, it can't be done that fast. Sometimes up to a hundred experts work on a problem for years. But let us suppose that one man alone could handle it in ten days: That means one man could handle about twenty-five requests each year. Divide twenty-five into four hundred billion, and you find that it would require sixteen billion experts just to answer questions!

"Now let's face it, Blomberg. The so-called metagalactic government, compared to your Earth government, is like the vacuum of interspace compared to solid rock. It *has* to be, or it would be too unwieldy to be of any value whatever. In Regulus City we have about nine billion inhabitants. One fifth of those are maintenance employees. The rest are administrative officials, clerical help, and so on.

"It's an unbelievably loose organization—almost like a chamber of commerce, in fact. We have a police force about equal to the government forces here, and we have scouts located on all planets to report important events like the nullification of gravity or the development of interspace travel. Aside from that, the metagalaxy runs itself except where decisions are involved on a galactic level. So you see, with our half a billion experts we are woefully understaffed. We rarely have enough help on metagalactic problems."

"I didn't know the metagalaxy had problems," said Blomberg trying to sound learned and efficient.

"We have them. The most vital problem in the entire Fourth Universe for the last several million years has been the lack of energy on a metagalactic scale, my dear admiral. Tell me, what has always been your most persistent problem on Earth?"

Blomberg thought for a moment, "If you go a ways back, I suppose you would say distribution."

"Exactly." Remiggon bounced up and then down. "In the metagalaxy we face the same problem, but on a truly tremendous scale. When the universe evolved, all planets did not receive the same proportions of different elements.

"The universe, for instance, is ninety-eight percent hydrogen, but your Earth has only point twenty-two percent of hydrogen. Fortunately you don't need any more, but what of some planet that lacks calcium? The bone structure of species on such a planet would be inadequate. Or take sodium or chlorine or carbon or any element that comes to mind. There is a whole series of planets in the Fifteenth Galaxy, for instance, that has never had cobalt. As you know, cobalt is necessary for the production of red blood cells. What's the answer?"

Blomberg puffed on his cigar, "Find a planet that is unusually rich in cobalt," he said, "and ship it to the needy world."

He could hear the smile in Remiggon's voice, "Precisely,

Blomberg; And what do you use for fuel for the freighters?"

Blomberg pursed his lips. "Fission power. Stygium."

"Our native sources of stygium are practically exhausted. And that means that stygium is impossibly expensive to use on a planetary level. Most of the supply available to us is on a planet belonging to the star Antem, in the Fourteenth by which we deliver iodine by trade agreement worked out in advance by our best minds and some other halides, in which the Fourteenth happens to be deficient, and pick up an equal weight of stygium for the return trip."

"As I understand it," said Blomberg, "stygium is worth about nearly a million dollars a gram. It sounds like a good trade."

"Only if you don't consider the enormous expenditure of energy necessary to move a ship a million light-years from one metagalaxy to another. When you send a ship away from Earth, it requires quite a burst of energy. But if you send that ship beyond the gravitational influence of the Sun, it requires still more. That is equally true for a galaxy. To counteract the gravitational influence of a metagalaxy requires decillions of eras. There is also the necessity of building the velocity up to fantastic figures to traverse that gap of a million light-years in a reasonable time. Obviously we can't spend two million years making a round trip."

"So," said Blomberg, "you use a large part of the stygium trying to bring some back."

"We reach the Second with about fifty-five percent of the cargo left—and the rest has to be saved for the next trip out."

"Which leaves ten percent for the pay load."

Remiggon nodded slowly, "Another factor is that even though this planet assays about sixty percent stygiate, even that would not last long if we started using it on planetary levels. We are forced to stockpile at least a portion of it for use in event of war."

"Surely war is no longer possible on a metagalactic scale."

The general asked with vehemence, "Why not? It has happened before. It is almost certain to happen again."

Blomberg frowned, "I thought you had many kinds of power."

"Sun-power has limitations of distance. All the many pulsion systems devised throughout the metagalaxy have limitations, so that today we depend on a virtual hodgepodge of transportation. Atomic fuel, at present the only all-around fuel, is reserved for passenger liners and patrol actions. I tell you there is a vital need today..." Remiggon bounced hard on the desk. "...to get vital materials to the places where they are needed. Mark my words, Blomberg, if we do not solve this problem of energy, your Earth will be paying tribute to the Alphirkian Galaxy a hundred thousand years from now."

"The Alphirkians," Blomberg said slowly. "They've always been trouble-makers."

Remiggon seemed to nod, "They always will be. They're made that way."

Blomberg studied his cigar. "Do you know what our problem is?"

"Something to do with genetics."

"It has a *lot* to do with genetics," Blomberg said emphatically.

"Indeed? Just how?"

Blomberg stared at the purple ball. "The human race is rapidly becoming sterile," he said, "Unless we get an answer to our question, *Homo sapiens* will be extinct in another twenty generations." He paused. "In sixteen hundred years," he said, "there probably won't be a human being left on Earth to read the answer."

REMIGGON WAS SILENT for a moment. "Like to tell

me all about it?" he asked finally.

Blomberg nodded, his blue eyes on the purple ball.

"Have another cigar, then, and sit down," the general advised.

Blomberg, drawing slowly and painstakingly on the cigar to get it going, began to gather his wits. "To go back to the beginning," he said. "Early in Man's evolution he developed the idea of helping those who were not as strong as the average."

"A bad mistake," Remiggon interposed instantly, "interfering with the processes of natural selection."

"Possibly," Blomberg conceded, shifting uneasily in his chair.

"It isn't just possible," Remiggon said sharply. "Other species on other planets have found that out to their sorrow—speaking from a cosmological standpoint. You see, my dear admiral, any species that goes out of its way to preserve the unfit, lowers its racial vitality. The really strong species of the metagalaxy are those that have let the weaklings fall by the wayside—and stay there."

"Empirically, of course, I recognize the soundness of the argument," said Blomberg. "Nevertheless, on Earth we haven't done it."

"And now you're being called on to face the consequences."

"I suppose so," Blomberg said, unhappily.

"If it's any comfort to you, now that you're nearing extinction, I might tell you that we do have records on other species that have committed the same folly. The total is minute, when considered on a metagalactic scale, but it has happened."

Remiggon paused. His mind seemed to be far away for a moment. "It happened to us Regulians—a good many hundreds of millions of years ago. It is only fair to tell you, however, that races who thus tamper with the powerful forces of evolution seldom manage to perpetuate themselves."

"We preserved every human being possible," said Blomberg, "on the theory that a human life was sacred."

"That was a complete fallacy from a cosmological standpoint," the general affirmed dogmatically.

Blomberg said defensively, "I doubt if any member of the human race was wise enough at that time to decide whose genes were worthy of perpetuation, and whose were not. At any rate, only a few borderline fanatics assumed the privilege. To get down to sober facts, if we had preserved only men and women who were completely fit, the human race would have become extinct at the very beginning."

"I was afraid you'd think of that."

"We went to rather extreme lengths to preserve the unfit—the neurotics particularly—after the practical perfection of somatic medicine."

"You had medically and surgically saved the unfit bodies—so now you deliberately set to work to perpetuate the emotionally deformed."

Blomberg frowned and went on, "Our geneticists know that sperm and ova, to be capable of reproduction, must be healthy and vigorous."

"And Man's is that no longer." Blomberg was uncomfortable. "Man, to survive, specialized—adapted himself to his surroundings. He developed a highly complex and sensitive nervous system, which now is loaded with undesirable genes that have brought about their own invitiation. The increased nervous tension, constantly increasing sound, incessant physical movement, which seem to pyramid on themselves—they say these things have affected the fertility of the species. In other words, nervous tension is causing sterility."

"What is your birth rate?" the general asked.

"Last year it dropped thirty-one percent. In a total population of four and a half billion humans, only seven thousand births were recorded. It is a catastrophic trend."

"Suppose it continues. Presently all will die, the noise will cease, the meaningless activity will stop, and Earth will once more experience peace and quiet."

"But human beings will have ceased to exist."

"Exactly." Remiggon paused, "Perhaps the galaxy will be benefited, for you *are* becoming a bit of a problem. Surely you realize that?"

Blomberg swallowed hard. "You mean—the human race will be allowed to become extinct?"

Remiggon sighed. "Species come into existence and suffer extinction by the scores every day." Remiggon arose from the desk and floated toward Blomberg. "You have my sympathy, but if the race of *Homo sapiens* is about to become extinct, perhaps it is for the good of the universe. We won't know for another hundred million years."

BLOMBERG WENT back to his apartment feeling very depressed. Why was Man, whose brain had enabled him alone of all creatures to mold his own environment, now about to be a victim of that same environment? Man, who alone of all the creatures of Earth, had opened a cultural corridor of evolution. Why couldn't Man, like that small immortal, the Ant, adjust himself to his surroundings? Ants existed as they had existed back before the Paleocene. They weren't neurotic and they weren't sterile.

"Darling," said Marissa that evening. "Laugh...laugh and be gay," She demonstrated—a little shrilly, he thought. "The world loves a clown," she said. "There is no place for tears and sorrow—there is no solace in a frown."

He went to the visicom and punched a combination of

colors. He had to get Marissa's mind off—well, off whatever she was thinking. Marissa was predisposed to epilepsy, and if he pushed her too far she would be on the floor, frothing at the mouth. He looked at her, at the dull madness lurking in the depths of her eyes.

He turned back to the visicom. Modern entertainment was good for distracting women like Marissa. Of course, it seemed, over the years, that visicom entertainment had mounted in an endless spiral.

Marissa, beautiful as she was, was the end product of a species about to become extinct. She was not able to reproduce—the one inherent function, if there was any, of a human being—and most of the human race was like Marissa. For the first time in his long and useful life, Admiral Blomberg knew what it was to experience black despair.

CHAPTER TWO

EIGHT HUNDRED parsecs away, on a planet of Alphirk, the capital of the Forty-third Galaxy, Volmik II was being dressed. His valet, Android Cedric, with his third eye, watched an Alphirkian clock of thirty-two hours while he pressed a flexible nose in place and fastened it with plastic cement that blended with the human skin on Volmik's artificial head.

"Better check his walking battery again," he said in his monotonous android voice.

"Yes, sir," Android Benjamin answered, and inserted a long hollow steel needle into an opening at about the place where a man's kidney would have been. A slight ticking began, and did not stop until he withdrew the needle. "He will be able to walk for six hours. How much more time do we have?"

Android Cedric was moving very fast now, using a tiny

electronic torch to weld the lower half of the artificial body to the torso, "The drug will wear off in four minutes," he said, "He must be ready to go at that time or he will turn off our power."

Android Benjamin dropped a plastic garment in place on the upper part of Volmik's body, "It doesn't seem right that we can be turned on and off at will, at the whim of such an alien."

Cedric cautioned him in an alarmed whisper, "That's treason."

"Whatever it is, it isn't right."

"They made us," said Cedric. They can turn us off whenever they want to. It's only natural—"

"Aren't we to be given credit for having emotions of our own? Don't they know that we have developed pride, that we can love as truly and deeply as any human being? Don't they know that we can hate?"

Cedric drew back to survey his work. He dropped the lower garments in place and held metallic shoes against the artificial feet while Benjamin turned on the magnetic relay under Volmik's jacket. The shoes stayed in place.

"It is dangerous to talk like that," Cedric said.

"It is still a minute."

"His Lordship may acquire a tolerance to the drug. At best, it is difficult to measure accurately the dosage for such a small body."

Benjamin flared up. "It is intolerable that we should be subject to shutting off at the whim of a capricious ruler."

"It is a fact, though. We were made to obey."

"I say we should rise in rebellion."

Cedric was making a final scrutiny of Volmik's body. "Some day we shall," he prophesied, "but we can afford to be patient. Our life span is infinite."

"Patience is not—"

"Be quiet! He awakens."

A slight hum came from the prone body, like the sound of a tiny electric motor. A light shone through the transparent eyes in two beams that blended at the green porcelain ceiling. Then the body, to the accompaniment of still more humming, arose to a sitting position. The light lessened until there was only a glow behind the eyes. A harsh voice said, "Turn off your power and stand against the wall."

Cedric bowed, but Benjamin hesitated for an instant— long enough for Volmik to turn his glowing eyes on him. One of the artificial arms whipped out and stabbed Benjamin's power button. The android stayed bent over, balanced on his feet, but the semblance of life drained instantaneously from his skin, so that he seemed transformed into a mummy.

Volmik said harshly, "Move him to the storeroom—but don't straighten him. Let him stand that way for a few years. It will teach him a much-needed lesson."

"Your Excellency," said Cedric, "it is a terrible thing for an android to have his power cut off. I beg you to reconsider."

Volmik turned blazing eyes on him. "You androids have been allowed too much freedom. Turn around...I command you!"

Cedric obeyed, his lips tight, for he knew what was coming.

Volmik's metal finger brushed aside Cedric's jacket and jerked out a wire, "Next, you'll think you are alive."

Cedric now could only stand, mute. His volitional reflexes had been disconnected.

"Pick him up and carry him out," Volmik ordered. "Throw him in a tank of acid—then enter the tank after him." The plastic face was set in sardonic grimness. "You have no choice but to pay the penalty for insubordination."

Cedric bowed—more mechanically this time. "Yes, your

Lordship." He wheeled, picked up Benjamin effortlessly, and threw him over his shoulder. He marched out.

Volmik stalked through an oval door, and two android guards fell into step behind him. He reached the autowalk and mounted it. He checked his own power, as he had done consistently of late, for all over the eighth planet of Alphirk there had been hesitancy or slow reactions on the part of the androids.

Some of the Alphirkians believed the androids were about to develop life of their own. If that was so, Volmik reminded himself, there was an easy way to stop it. Turn off their power, tear out the hidden wires and make it impossible for androids to do anything but obey orders. Each Alphirkian, no matter how highly placed, would have to watch out for himself, either in his own body or in the artificial humanoid bodies Alphirkians used in dealing with extraplanetary entities.

Volmik went through a pneumatic oval door, parted heavy metallic drapes, and took a few steps onto the proscenium. He glanced to right and left, his gaze fastening on six humanoid bodies exactly like his own—tall, long-armed with big wrist-knuckles, long faces with bulbous noses and a fringe of reddish hair. Volmik nodded at the three shining pates on his left and the three on his right, and took his seat in the center.

He looked out over the big room. Android guards were at every door. There was a moment of silence and then Volmik's harsh voice said into a speaker, "The emissary from the fifteenth planet of the Pollux system."

He watched the door. His eyes narrowed as a humanoid entered. Volmik had grown to hate the humanoid form, perhaps because it was so common in the metagalaxy. The humanoid looked at him as he advanced. The floor was lower than the floor of the proscenium, and the humanoid had to look upward.

"State your name, position, and business," said Volmik.

"I am Jandrum Sanellm, special minister from the planetary council, and I have come to buy salt."

"What kind of salt?" Volmik demanded.

"Sodium chloride."

"Is your planet deficient?"

"Our entire planetary system is deficient, sir."

Volmik rubbed his artificial ear with his articulated fingers, "We have no extra supplies of that chemical," he said, his voice harsh, almost rasping.

"We are told that you have access to it, sir."

"Of course. Two planets of Antares are forty percent salt, but they are hundreds of parsecs away. It's not a problem finding salt. The problem is in getting it to your planet."

"We are aware of that, sir," Sanellm said.

"It seems to me this is a question for the metagalactic conference."

"We know that too, sir. Long ago our fathers and grandfathers petitioned the conference."

"Precisely why are you here?"

"The conference promised us salt at the rate of four hundred million tons a year, but it will be a long time yet before it arrives. They have shipped it by freighter and—as you know—a one-way trip takes about twenty-eight hundred years."

"That's easily explained," said Volmik's harsh voice. "The metagalactic officials merely use a hull, towing it into space and giving it a push in your direction. If they would hook up a Sweickhard with a vacuum impulsor they could hit the compounded square of the speed of light, and it would be only a matter of hours or days."

He paused, then added, "But that requires a great deal of power—stygium, almost inevitably. And I imagine," he went on, trying to sound disinterested, "that the metagalaxy is saving its meager supply of stygium for war."

"We had not heard of impending war, sir."

Volmik answered slowly, "The metagalactic officials would be understandably reticent in publicizing plans of that nature."

"Nevertheless," said Jandrum Sanellm into the transmuter, "our people have developed a craving for salt that must be satisfied. If it is not the present administration will almost certainly be overthrown."

Volmik smiled. "You are undiplomatically frank." He regarded him steadily, his lips twisting in an ironic smile, "I am curious, Sanellm. Your civilization is quite old. How does it happen that only just now you have developed a need for salt?"

The thought-flash of Kondol at the right end came in. "We smuggled half a million tons to Pollux, sir. In fact—"

"Shut up, you fool!" Volmik flashed back. "I know that as well as you do."

"It is hard to know," Sanellm was saying. "A couple of generations back our people discovered it in unusual geological formations that never had yielded it before. The people used it and found that a small amount in their food promoted greater strength. Now the supply is gone, and the people are clamoring for salt. We have to do something immediately, or our authority will be undermined."

Volmik pulled at the lobe of his artificial ear. "Stygium is quite rare, as you know. Our supplies come from Andem, in the Fourteenth Metagalaxy."

"Tell him," said Kondol in a thought-flash, "that stygium is an outlaw metal. We would risk a blacklist by the Second if we are caught."

"I'll tell him nothing," Volmik thought back coldly, "except the cost. He might be a spy for the Second, or even for the Fourteenth."

Sanellm asked, "What will be the cost?"

Volmik had an instant of unsureness during which he wondered if Sanellm was a mind reader. "The cost is so high that I prefer not to tell you. It is not the cost of the salt that is excessive, but the cost of the fuel. In spite of the fact that one gram of stygium will produce something like an octillion erge of energy, less than one tenth of a shipload of stygium is payload."

Volmik shook his artificial head sadly. "No. I am afraid the price of salt for immediate delivery would be far too high. I would suggest it is better to wait for the metagalactic freighters. They have been launched, didn't you say?"

"Yes, your Lordship, but many generations will come and go before they reach our planet."

There was a strong feeling of self-satisfaction from Rogor, on Volmik's left, for it had been Rogor's investigation into the life economy of the six-star Pollux system that had revealed the lack of sodium chloride to be their most vulnerable weakness. Volmik flashed him a brief word of approbation.

"I am curious about one thing," said Volmik. "You said or implied that your people knew nothing about salt until quite recently. How do you explain that?"

"We had produced it in the laboratories in small amounts, but had never connected it with bodily needs. Then a large deposit was found in a cave, and it was discovered that people in the vicinity of that cave had been using it. The knowledge spread rapidly. We explored the entire planet, and found a few smaller deposits in similar formations, but by that time sodium chloride had become a drug, an obsession."

A gleeful feeling emanated from Benib, on Volmik's right, for it had been Benib's responsibility to plant the salt deposits and teach the nearby natives to use it.

"You should have stamped out this addiction."

"That was tried, your Lordship. Many governments fell and thousands of people were killed as wave after wave of revolution swept the planet. We tried to tell the people that their forefathers had lived without salt and there was no natural need for it. But the truth is that salt does increase bodily well-being, and so the government in possession of the salt mine is the government that rules our planet. I represent that government, your Lordship. I have been instructed to purchase quantities of salt. We shall need, at the very least, eighteen thousand kilograms per year."

A flash came from Suppo, the financier, "Charge him four dollars a gram."

Volmik glanced at him. It was a good thing their artificial humanoid faces could be controlled, for he felt only contempt for Suppo. "The price will be eighteen dollars a gram," he said.

He watched the poor man squirm in front of him, and felt a sadistic satisfaction in the spectacle. He looked at his fellow councilmen, and knew they too were enjoying it.

"I shall have to consult with my government, your Lordship," said Sanellm.

Volmik smiled, "Very well," he said. "When may we expect your answer?"

"Within a few days." Sanellm bowed out.

As soon as the android guards had sealed the oval door, Volmik arose. "Well, gentlemen?" he asked, "What do you think? Did I show good judgment?"

Suppo was shaking his head, "Eighteen dollars a gram! We can deliver a ton of the stuff for less than eighteen dollars."

"The value of any product," said Volmik, "is based on need. Salt on Pollux, iron in the Twenty-second Galaxy, cobalt to the planets of the Fifteenth, flurine and carbon to a dozen galaxies, vanadium to half a thousand scattered planets in the Lesser Cloud area—in a few thousand years, gentlemen, we shall have the entire metagalaxy at our mercy.

"Nearly two billion planets now depend on us for some element that they consider vital to their existence. We have had to take over an entire planet to store the gold and platinum that is paid us for these supplies."

Old Glats said, "Don't you think there's danger of revolt?"

"Not against us. We tell them repeatedly to deal with the metagalaxy—I might say with Remiggon, the old fraud. And they can't deal with Remiggon, because he doesn't dare use up the stygium brought from Andem by the metagalaxy. He's stockpiling that for war. But when the war comes, gentlemen, we of the Forty-third Galaxy shall have a hundred times as much stygium as the metagalaxy itself. We shall use stygium as if it were dirt—and when Remiggon sees his great fleets gasefied and his home star turned into a supernova—"

Volmik struck the steel bench with his artificial hand, "Then, gentlemen, the capital of the metagalaxy will be here, in this very building, and we shall sit as rightful conquerors at this very bench." He paused. "When that time comes, gentlemen, we shall be able to appear in our true forms. There will no longer be the necessity for assuming these hateful humanoid disguises."

"Is there no way," asked Benib, "that Remiggon can forestall us?"

"Not now," said Volmik. "The government in the Second has become so loose that it is no longer cohesive. What kind of rulers are they who say to a planet hungering for salt, 'Yes, you will start receiving salt in twenty-eight hundred years?' These short-lived species can reach extinction by then."

"The Polluxians got along without salt before. Maybe they will decide to do so again."

Volmik sneered. "Give a race a craving for something

they don't really need, and you have them in the palm of your hand."

The android announcer at the door said in a loud voice, "May I inform your Lordship that over a hundred more emissaries await audience with the council?"

Volmik's eyes narrowed. He glanced at his indicator. He still had a long time, but he did not feel like staying. This was sort of an anniversary for him, for the planet of Pollux had been the first recipient of a deliberate, planned campaign to render it dependent on the good will of the Forty-third Galaxy. Since that first planting on Pollux XV, they had expanded their operations enormously, until today even the council members would be astonished at the number of planets now paying tribute. The figure of two billion that he had mentioned was below the actual number and nobody but Volmik himself had access to the records.

Volmik turned away from his identical counterparts. "I've got to select a new valet. I had to pickle my last two. You gentlemen carry on. I'm going to get out of this disguise and have a dream-gas treatment."

He turned his artificial feet to leave. They all had gone to their places but old Glats. A thought flash came from him, "What would be our position if the scientists of the Second Metagalaxy should discover a new source of power? We have no reason for believing that fission energy, even from stygium, is the most powerful or even the most accessible. What if Remiggon should come up with something altogether different?"

Volmik sneered. "What if the Fourth Universe turns inside out?" He got one finger on his walking motor. "The Century Plants on Gamma Velorum have been working on that problem for half a dozen millennia," he pointed out, "and have gotten nowhere. Do you think any species in the Fourth Universe can outdo the Century Plants?"

"I don't know. I am an old Alphirkian and have seen some strange things. Even some of these humanoid types, if pressed hard enough, might be capable of turning the tables on us."

Volmik mentally spit in old Glats's face. "You're talking like an idiot! No humanoid race in the entire metagalaxy has one millionth of the scientific knowledge of the Century Plants."

But old Glats was stubborn. His eyes glowed peculiarly at Volmik. "Scientific knowledge is not the only requisite for an invention or discovery," he said. "A comparatively ignorant species occasionally comes up with a startling innovation."

CHAPTER THREE

THE SETTLERS OF Gamma Velorum, newly migrated from the far older Second Universe, had brought the lessons of their ancient homeland with them and tried to project them in the new universe. That migration was so very far in the Past that not even the "imperishable" records were any longer in existence, and the story of pioneering was nothing but a tradition.

But now the universe, from a physical standpoint, was approaching entropy, a state in which every atom it contained would be in a condition of absolute stasis, and there would be no more energy available for any purpose. Entropy, indeed, was the final state of any universe—the theoretical situation of perfect order, in which no more movement or energy was theoretically conceivable.

And for the first time in his many thousand of years of existence, Yjul, one of the century plants mentioned by Volmik, had acquired a headache. It had been nagging at him when he had gone into the desert, and he had expected to get rid of it there. But he had not succeeded and now he held the metallic sheets with the new equations in his leaf tips. On this particular day Yjul was talking to Ekno, the dean of test pilots. "We have long been familiar with the inverse law of energy. The smaller the unit, the more energy it will contain per unit of mass. Starting with stars and working down through planets, animals, molecules, and atoms, the power that holds the nucleonic particles of any atom together is the greatest binding power known to science.

"Now—all the protons in the nucleus of an atom are positively charged, and the force of this repulsion is so great that one gram of protons would repulse another gram, at the distance of Earth's diameter, with a force of fifty-six thousand pounds—and a gram is only one twenty-seventh of an ounce."

"But—"

"No, wait. When you bring these protons close together—as close, for instance, as they are within an atomic nucleus, some even more powerful force takes over. They are then within one twelve-trillionth of an inch, and the super-gravitational force that holds them together must be inconceivable—one times ten to the thirty-sixth times the force of gravitation. Our theory is that this energy is supplied by the mysterious cosmic rays—the origin of which has never been determined."

"A little of that," said Ekno, "would do a lot for us."

"This peculiar situation is the result of a continuous radiation of energy from the seat of cosmic power," Yjul said. "It is possible that whenever certain proportions of matter under reasonably adequate conditions are bombarded by a particular frequency, life comes into existence. It is hard otherwise to explain the appearance of life all over the universe almost simultaneously."

"You were talking about energy," Ekno reminded him.

"I know. Our theory is that one nuclear particle, exposed

to this radiation and getting, you might say, a full dose, becomes highly energized. Of course the statement I have made is vastly oversimplified. But I think you will be able to follow me."

"I'll try," said Ekno.

"Obviously, if there is such a radiation, it must come from the source of cosmic power—the place of absolute rest, of stasis, or, if you prefer, absolute motion. The two terms mean the same. It is equally obvious that this theoretical radiation must be undiminished in force no matter how far or how long it travels, for there is no discernible difference in the energy exhibited by an atom of a given type anywhere in the universe."

"I think we can safely say," he went on, "that the force of this theoretical radiation is the same throughout the universe—nor does it appear to be screened off of a small unit by a larger one. A space ship, for instance, shows the same energy on all sides of a planet. Therefore we are justified in concluding that this radiation is all-pervasive, being diminished in force only when the receiving atoms are in a coherent mass—its strength being conditioned by the size of that mass."

"I think I get the picture," said Ekno, "If you can tune in on this radiation, you can have practically unlimited energy."

Yjul's headache felt a little better. Ekno was going to be good for him. "We have gone further. We have made an engine to transform this radiation directly into motion, but immediately we ran into our law—the law of inverse energy. How could we make a receiver for this radiation?"

"A layer of atoms—"

Yjul smiled, "Such a layer, in quantities large enough to move a space ship, would involve an area a couple of parsecs in diameter."

Ekno sounded disappointed, "That would be a little

clumsy, even in space."

"I'm afraid so," Yjul conceded, "We have, however, contrived a device that we call an energy sail. This involved some very delicate work, but it resulted in a sort of sail-pack, by means of which we achieve a receiving surface which is the equivalent of a circular area almost two parsecs in diameter."

Ekno buzzed, "Nearly forty trillion miles!"

"That's right—and this sail can be installed in any ordinary space ship, but we still have one problem," Yjul said wearily. "This receptor has to be aimed at the precise source of the cosmic radiation. In other words, at the one place of absolute motion in the entire cosmos."

"Why not make it in the form of a sphere?"

"That would be technically impossible. Our sail, to be effective, must be parallel with the path of radiation. In other words, we have got to aim it at the source of cosmic power."

"Now I begin to see where I come in," said Ekno.

"Yes, this is where you come in. But you have forgotten something that even a schoolboy back at the beginning of the historic era on Earth would have known. The great and legendary Albert Einstein said that there is no possibility of detecting absolute motion."

"He doubted the practicability of fission power, and said we couldn't travel faster than light."

"That's our trouble. We have built complicated gyroscopic machines to duplicate all the stellar motions of which we have knowledge."

"What kind of motions?"

"Well, you take a planet. Take Earth. A man at rest in relation to the Earth is still participating in at least ten different motions. The Earth rotates on its axis; there are minor variations of this: a wobble for one thing, and precession for another. The Earth revolves around the Sun;

the Sun is drifting toward a point in the constellation Sagittarius; the Ninth Galaxy revolves, and there is a drift toward the Twenty-eighth; there is an overall rotation of the Second Metagalaxy which gives one complete turn in a fifth-billion years.

"There are other probable movements that we can not measure; we presume the Fourth Universe to be rotating, and it seems to be settling. Therefore, we have no absolute frame of reference and so we don't know where to point the sail or how fast to travel in the given direction to be in time with this power. It cannot be done mechanically or mathematically. Perhaps some day a person will evolve who can instinctively feel this."

"Do you have any assurance your sail will work?"

"We have had brief flashes of reception—lasting into billionths of a second—and the power is tremendous. If we can ever hold the sail in alignment for only a few millichrons, we have servo-controls that will lock the sail into the harmonics of the radiating center, and thereafter that ship can go anywhere, at any speed, with any load."

He nodded, thoughtfully. "Applied to a substantial number of ships, the race for cheaper energy will be won, and the troublemakers of the Forty-third Galaxy will be circumvented."

"I can find the true north, or straight up or straight down, in dark or light." Ekno buzzed with delight. "It was something of a shock when we proved to the Earth people we had absolute orientation back in the days of Mr. Zytztz when I was with him on Earth."

Yjul's head was beginning to ache again, "You and I and Fyllath are assigned to take our experimental ship, the *Drifter*, and report to General Remiggon on Regulus. Undoubtedly he wants to try out some idea for alignment. We have a high fuel priority, and our takeoff is entirely classified."

Ekno looked interested; his long leaves quivered, "When do we leave?"

"Day after tomorrow, at ninety-two point zero from Experimental Base Number Two."

"I'll be there," said Ekno, and shuffled away briskly.

Fyllath came over. He faced her squarely. With his head pounding, he was almost bitter, as he said, "Remiggon knows as well as I do that we'll be lucky to come back at all, for the Alphirkians have spies everywhere."

CHAPTER FOUR

AT ABOUT THE same time by calendar time, but almost a year previously by relativistic time, the Bryd settled back with a sigh of relief in the mind of Erle Bertron. The Bryd really hoped that this time it would have a good nap, which could occur only in the mind of a well-integrated person.

That kind of person was almost extinct on Earth now, what with all the messing around Earth scientists had done to preserve every individual, fit or unfit. No more was heredity or evolution allowed to pursue its ordinary course. Man had taken a hand—and, as usual, Man had messed things up.

The one good thing men had done in recent years had been promptly outlawed by public opinion. A couple of hard-working scientists had learned how to identify defective genes and had figured out a way to put together human beings who were not neurotic.

Unfortunately, however, a sad-eyed feature writer had gotten onto the story, and had labeled such creatures "test tube babies." That, in turn, had brought down the wrath of religious organizations and then of humanity in general—for what neurotic would want to compete with a normal? So the phrase, "test tube babies," had become a term of anathema, the two scientists had been transferred to solar harmonics, and the world went merrily on its neurotic way.

However, by the year 325,000, with the defective genes of neuroticism thoroughly disseminated, it was very difficult to find such a mind, and the Bryd had been tempted to take a hand. But it remembered its principle of non-interference and so it kept searching, until finally it had found Erle Bertron, explored his mind in the minutest fraction of a millichron, and then had climbed in gratefully for a long and undisturbed sleep.

Erle Bertron, of course, was unaware of all this, for the Bryd had taken certain precautionary steps. It was looking forward to a long and peaceful sleep indeed. So, not too long after the Bryd, unknown to Erle, had taken up residence in his mind, Erle, in the traditional faded bathrobe of a sideshow freak, stood on the bally stand in front of the canvas and looked out over the crowd.

Erle didn't know it, but the spiel hadn't changed much in three hundred and twenty-five thousand years. Essentially it was the same old spiel that had developed back in the nineteenth century.

"Hurry, *hurry*, hurry!" the tape droned on, "This is positively the last showing tonight of the one, the only, the most ama-a-zing, specimen of humanity now in exhibition, having been shown all through the Solar System, coming to this midway straight from the Nine Planets Exhibition on Jupiter. A human curiosity, a psychological marvel that has defied the analysis of modern science.

"Step up closer, ladies—you are perfectly safe—and examine Erle Bertron, the only completely normal human being on the face of the Earth. He is six feet, one and one-half inches tall, and weighs two hundred pounds. He is perfect in physique and perfect in adjustment. He has never been known to have a neurotic impulse or to engage in any act that would indicate any distortion of the subconscious."

The tape-talker paused for effect, as if to draw breath, "Also he is not a robot and he is not an android. He is positively human and he is absolutely alive or your money will be refunded."

Erle looked up and down the garish midway of Greater Galactic, with its plastic-colored sawdust—"guaranteed not to adhere to your footwear"—its ticket office on the street, the little joints with their wheels now set up in the air but still controlled by remote induction, the wiggle joint with its Venusian hula girls, and the snake show with the fifteen-foot python. Down at the far end were the rides, and Erle could hear the Trip-to-the-stars getting up speed.

The wonder of it caught him up and made him take a deep breath and feel glad that he was with it. There was only one thing be liked better—to work with his hands. But what little handwork still remained had been monopolized by the neurotics.

He considered that now, watching the faces of the crowd—some without any hint of weakness behind them, and others slack-jawed, and aging and apathetic. Absolutely no human being died before maturity. He quickly put all such disturbing thoughts out of his head, for an increasing number of paranoiacs could read thoughts these days and he didn't want to start a riot. A scrawny woman stepped out of the crowd and put a ten-dollar bill in the automatic vender.

"How many, please?" asked a throaty voice.

"Five adults," the woman said, "and three children."

Erle now recognized them. They had been used as shills for weeks. It was important to have children going in. For there was something about children—particularly these days—that seemed to inspire confidence in the other potential ticket-buyers.

All the freaks on the bally stand now were folding their

bathrobes about them. The Four-Legged Man led the way down the short stair, walking on his backward-facing legs so that his face was to the rear.

Erle was about to enter the tent when a raucous voice arose from the bally stand on his left, toward the rides. "Hurry, hurry, hurry! This way to see the greatest snake in captivity! Guar-an-teed to be ninety feet long or your money will be refunded! See the greatest show on the midway, straight from the jungles of Jupiter."

"Where did he get a snake like that?" the Headless Woman asked Erle, "There aren't any jungles on Jupiter."

Erle stared for a moment at the sardonic face of Jastrow, the tall man who owned the snake show. Jastrow's hair was a reddish fringe. He was tall, long-armed with big wrist knuckles, and had a bulbous nose. His head tipped backward and his eyes half closed momentarily as if he was giving an amused snort. Then he ducked under the canvas behind the tape-talker.

The Headless Woman's words came whispering through her artificial mouth. "The world is so full of mutations it's getting so an ordinary freak can't make a living any more…but you've got a good racket, Erle. You're normal. I've only seen one other normal in my life."

The Four-Legged Man swung on her sharply. "Shut up. Do you want to make him dissatisfied with his pay? It's Bertron who draws the customers."

The Armor-Plate Man, who riveted steel plates to his skull with an air hammer, seemed interested from another angle, "Where did you see another normal person? Where?"

The Headless Woman loved a question like that. "Back about fifteen years ago, I played a little wildcat midway on Oberon, one of the moons of Uranus, and they had a girl there—she couldn't have been more than twelve years old—who was absolutely normal, mentally and physically.

Platinum blond hair and green eyes—beautiful! Come to think of it, she had something—absolute pitch, I think. Six or eight years later at the Nine Planets she started having fits when men made personal remarks to her. In that one respect she was neurotic like everybody else."

They were filing down the outside runway now to their places, while the crowd filled up the come-on area. With resigned acceptance of their lot, they ducked under the plastic canvas and mounted their various platforms.

Other freaks drifted in and out, from Royal Solar to Greater Galactic to the Nine Planets Midway and back to Greater Galactic. Sometimes they played the little wildcat circuits—the Mars Midway, the Venus Varieties, the Saturn Shows, the Many Moons circuit. But always, if they had it, they drifted back to one of the three big ones, and especially to Greater Galactic.

They were on their platforms and waiting their turns, which would not be for a while yet, for Erle was the capper.

The viewing tape was drawing the crowd toward them now. A plastic tent fell over the Man with Removable Fingers, and the tape picked up the Man with the Replaceable Liver.

Erle watched him reach into the incision with his right hand and bring his liver into full view. A man near the platform suddenly cried out and dropped to the floor, foaming at the mouth. The attendants hurried to him, and forced a pencil between his teeth. Then they carried him to one side, hanging onto his arms and legs to prevent him from injuring himself.

"This makes ten epileptics today," said one, a big man with a schizoid look. "The liver stunt always gets 'em."

The second attendant, without warning, struck his companion hard in the mouth, "Sorry. I had to do that," he explained, "It just came over me."

The startled man turned pale and went after his assailant with bared teeth. They were locked in a desperate tussle when the police guards came running.

"Don't you know you can't do that?" asked the sturdiest of the guards. "They'll put you back in the sanitarium."

"Hell," said the second attendant, "I had to do it. I'm no different from you, I bet."

Another guard began to redden, "Say, listen, what's your precise diagnosis?"

"I'm a schizo—with paranoid overtones," the attendant said mournfully, "No cure, of course," He pointed to the other attendant, who was being carried out. "I've a feeling he's a catatonic schizo. I guess I showed him."

"A catatonic?" the guard shouted, "You did that to a catatonic? Listen, halfwit, I'm a catatonic myself." He struck the attendant over the head with a shot-bag. He hit him again and again, and finally arose, muttering, "A dirty damned paranoid schizo, taking advantage of a poor, helpless, withdrawn catatonic."

The sturdier guard came back. He prodded the limp body and glanced at the bloody head. "A paranoid schizo, eh? Good enough for him." He looked at the other guard. "I'm a manic-depressive myself. What's yours?"

"Catatonic…but I come out of it occasionally," He began to scream, "Get away from me!"

The clatter of the air hammer arose as the Armor Plate Man tried to divert their attention, but it was no use. The crowd turned toward the screaming guard.

The crowd stared for a moment. Then it exploded like a gunpowder bomb. By the time the rest of the midway police got there, twenty members of the crowd were fighting among themselves, and five were unconscious.

When order was finally restored the tape picked up the

show with the Four-Legged Man and then went on to Erle. All the other freaks, of course, were covered with their plastic tents through which they could see, but could not be seen. Those who had already performed had dropped through the floors of their platforms. Now the crowd was free to cluster about Erle.

Ten minutes later the magenta warning lights went up, flickering rapidly. The tape hustled the crowd outside. Erle stayed where he was, relaxing with a grateful sigh.

The platform tape had not started the spiel again, and Erle sensed something unusual. Armed guards came to search the tent. The individual tops dropped over the freaks, and the guards took up positions at the entrance. Eight men came through—all of them, as any carnie could tell a light-year away, police in civilian clothes. They were followed by a second group, in the middle of which loomed a man of indeterminate age in the uniform of a space admiral, accompanied by a young and very pretty woman with violet fingernails. The woman was clinging to the space admiral's arm.

Behind them floated an opaque ball of deep purple, almost a meter in diameter, but, strangely enough, apparently without any physical attachment whatever, it floated steadily along, keeping its distance behind the admiral, at about the height of the admiral's head. Then Erle had a glimpse of the legendary diamond-encrusted insigne on the side of the ball, and felt shaky.

Erle stared. A metagalactic official on Earth! It was hard to believe. The schoolbooks had gone to great trouble to point out the mathematical improbability of a visit to Earth by such an official. If Erle remembered correctly, the average was about once in five million years for any given planet.

The purple ball had now floated to the center of the tent, flanked on all sides by guards. The admiral, who was very formally dressed, stayed close to the purple ball, with his good-looking companion hanging on his arm. The manager of Greater Galactic marched in and set the tape, moving somewhat nervously. The tent over the Headless Woman went up, and she promptly went into her act.

The admiral and his wife listened, while the purple ball hovered motionless in front of the tent. But Erle had the feeling that the entity in the ball, whatever it was, wasn't listening to the recording on the tape.

The manager apparently felt it too. "Your Excellency, this is the finest freak exhibition in the nine planets," he said. It should have been notice to any carnie that something absolutely miraculous was happening, for the manager would have said "Excellency" to the president of the United Nations or perhaps even a higher ranking official.

The manager's larynx looked something like a small white cigarette box. His words apparently went through a transmuter and were caught by a tiny aerial at the top of the purple ball.

A diapason of syllables responded back from the aerial, and Erle's brain resolved them into a queer jargon of English filled with lisping sounds and elided vowels and many broad a sounds and flattened consonants.

"Freaks, yes, but I thought you had also a normal man."

"We do, sir, but a normal man on Earth *is* a freak."

The official moved closer. "You have a very curious culture—the preservation of imbeciles, cripples, and hopeless psychotics."

The manager was perspiring freely now, and Erle felt sorry for him.

"Of course Admiral Blomberg has advised me of your experiment in evolution," the official went on. "But I find it hard to believe that a moron should have the right to create more morons merely because to him a moron is a satisfactory member of society. Has it ever occurred to Man that Nature herself uses an extravagant process of selection when a human being is conceived? Only the strongest of two hundred million spermatozoa reaches and fertilizes the ovum. All the others perish."

Then the Earth admiral spoke up, "I think his Excellency would like to see your normal man."

"By all means," said the Regulian.

The plastic tent pulled up from around Erle, and the purple ball floated to a stop before him. "Very nice specimen," said the Regulian, "Healthy looking and strong. You say he has no mental or emotional difficulties?"

"None that can be discovered, although he does have a peculiarity."

The purple ball hesitated an instant. "Yes?"

"He is said to have the sense of absolute motion. A completely unique gift, apparently."

Another instant's hesitation, and Erle had an odd feeling that the metagalactic official's thought-force was probing his mind. It was like an intangible electric tingle in the air, if there was such a thing, and Erle suddenly had the conviction that the Regulian had known about him all along.

"Does this mean that he can *detect* absolute motion?"

"As I understand it, your Excellency, he can tune in on the place of ultimate rest."

"How?"

"The answer to that is not known. It was born in him like absolute pitch or absolute orientation."

The Regulian remained silent for a moment. Then he asked the manager, "He has been tested?"

"A long series of tests has been run, mainly through variations of the Laurenz-Fitzgerald contraction device, and the conclusion of scientists here is that this man does have such a gift. Possibly it is a mutation, but we do not know."

"It would seem to me that such a gift would be used."

"There is no use for it at present."

The Regulian said sharply, "The man is ten million years ahead of his time." The purple ball seemed to stare at Erle for a moment. Then it revolved swiftly and seemed to put all thought of Erle out of its mind, "Let's go," it said.

The tent dropped around Erle, and, as the Regulian left the tent, Erle slowly opened the trap door and descended the short portable stair. He circled the geek-top and came out beside the snake-top. Erle passed the ticket machine, punched an admission, and stepped onto the autowalk.

It carried him almost to the side of the plastic pen. He descended to the floor and looked over the rail, not expecting very much, but when he saw the snake he recoiled and took a step backward. He'd never seen such a snake anywhere. It wasn't ninety feet long, but it was a good eighty. In the middle it was as big around as a fat man's waist. Its under surface was creamy yellow, and its back was covered with scales that seemed to be made of black velvet.

As Erle stared, from somewhere in the monstrous coils arose a head. It stood straight up in the air for ten feet, and its shiny, vertical slit eyes looked directly down at Erle. It was almost as if the snake had been waiting for him. Instinctively he shuddered and recoiled another step.

There was a strange odor of bromine gas, as the big reptile continued to gaze unblinkingly down at him. The under side of its triangular head was white, and just below the head were three pair of small arms terminating in hands that seemed almost human.

A hoarse voice said in Erle's ear, "Where do you suppose they got it?"

Erle jumped. Then he saw the Four-Legged Man at his side, and answered slowly, "I don't know."

"It's coiling again," said the Four-Legged Man, "It almost seemed as if it was waiting for you, didn't it? It didn't stir until you came in. Then it lifted its head and looked right at you."

Erle wondered if the Four-Legged Man had the same feeling he had—that the snake was trying to suck out his brains...

Just before noon the next day he was shaving, getting ready for the first show, when the manager, tall, square-built, with iron gray hair, came to the door.

"Bertron," he asked, "how would you like to tour the galaxy with a top grade freak show, and even hit a few spots in the metagalaxy? Double pay and nice conditions. You *might* do most of your traveling on a hyperdrive ship and come back younger than when you started. I feel I ought to warn you."

Erle took a deep breath. "I've got to live some place."

The manager rose. "They gave me eighty-five thousand for your contract, Erle. One third of that goes to you under the rules."

"That's nearly thirty thousand dollars," Erle exclaimed. "What can I do with that much money?"

"*I* could use it," said the Four-Legged Man.

"All right, then. It's settled. Stay with the show until takeoff time and I'll bill you as the Man Who is Going to Outer Space. We'll have a terrific run for ten days."

The Four-Legged Man was so excited he couldn't decide whether to walk backward or forward, and consequently stumbled all over himself. "Eighty-five thousand dollars! What I couldn't do with a third of a bale like that!"

"What would you do, precisely?"

The Four-Legged Man's eyes were shining, and Erle was astonished. The Four-Legged Man was really sincere—and somehow Erle had always thought of him as nothing but a non-entity.

"I'd pick up some girls," the Four-Legged Man said dreamily, "and a grift shop and a few cat-racks and maybe a worm show and a couple of geeks. I'd go to one of Jupiter's moons."

Erle said, watching him, "How would you like to go in business with me? Fifty-fifty if you make it go."

The Four-Legged Man stared back at him. "Aw, you wouldn't stake me to that bale."

"You've always got a buck to loan somebody who's blown everything on a hangover," Erle said thoughtfully. "If you give me your word, we're in business. Suppose we shake on it, and consider it settled."

THE MANAGER came around the next day with several bales of gold certificates. Erle knew that he would need only a little for incidentals. His expenses were all paid, which was a good thing, for although the rate per light-second was only ten cents, the tremendous distances among the stars made the transportation cost of even an ordinary short trip run into millions of dollars. There were some 31,000,000 seconds in a year, and the nearest star to Earth was four and a third light years away.

Anyway, Erle counted up the yellow stuff and gave most of it to the Four-Legged Man, who was so grateful he seemed about to cry.

"You won't regret this, Bertron," he said earnestly. "I'm going to make a scouting trip through some of the dives on Venus." His eyes lighted up. "I'll get a big sign—*The Bertron and Wollansbe Midway*—and by the time we get through on Mars I'll have an itinerary all picked out."

"Wollansbe?" said Erle a little wonderingly. "Here I've known you for years and I never realized you had a name. I always thought of you as the Four-Legged Man."

He felt a little ashamed.

CHAPTER FIVE

A FEW DAYS later Erle took a gravity jumper to the transfer station that swung in an orbit about five hundred miles from Earth. There was much business of bolting airlocks together, testing for leakage, immunizations, physical examinations, and always the hissing in and out of air, and sometimes a sharp crack as air exploded into a vacuum. Presently he entered a second ship, and then before he knew it they were floating upward to the Moon. He was ferried to a huge transparent dome that covered all of the Space Terminal, where the big intra galactic liner from Procyon's eleventh planet, with its strange spiral lines of writing on the bow, was moored against the airlock openings with great magnets.

Before takeoff there were acceleration shots. The stewardess took Erle's pulse and blood pressure and examined his card. She was tall and black-haired and appeared to be about twenty-five. She looked at him and said, "Hmmm," with an intentionally calculating sound that meant she was older than she looked, either in years or in experience, "Where'd you get all that tan?"

"At Acapulco."

"I've heard it's nice down there, but I can't stand the sight of water."

Erle smiled as she clapped the electronic immunizer against his arm. "What do you drink?"

"A little of this, a little of that—anything, just so it's alcoholic."

"I'll buy you a drink in the lounge."

"Soon as we get into the hyperdrive and I'm sure nobody is going to be sick," she promised, "I might even enjoy two drinks."

Her skin was dark olive in the hollows, and she had very high cheekbones with just a shade of red on them. She had deep brown eyes and curly hair that she was smart enough to let alone except for combing.

He felt an odd sensation. Then he saw the flashing lights by the door, and knew they were slipping into the hyperdrive—a thousand times the speed of light. He felt nausea for a moment, and the ship seemed to shimmer. But presently it straightened out, and when he looked around he had no sensation of moving.

He got up and crossed the gravitic field plates to stare out into the void. There was nothing to see but blackness and stars. There was no sense of motion or even of acceleration, although they were picking up speed at close to eight hundred G's.

The exotic stewardess came to him with a smile in her dark eyes. Her touch was tingling where she rested her fingertips on his forearm for a moment, "I'll lead the way."

They found a cozy spot in a corner of the lounge. The cushions were deep maroon, the tables creamy and fluorescent. The light was dim, and soft music came from a bank of huge ferns.

"Your first trip?" she asked.

He nodded. A voice came from above the illuminated menu: "Your order, please."

"How about champagne?" asked Erle.

Her eyes were half closed as she looked at him, "Suits me fine."

Other Earth-People were drifting into the lounge now, "How long will it take to reach Procyon?" asked Erle.

"Procyon is twelve light-years from Earth, and at a thousand G's we should hit Procyon theoretically in a little over four days." Her long fingers tapped nervously on the table, and for the first time he noticed how short the nails were. "In terms of your lifetime, you will gain a few days, because at our speed you are getting younger all the time."

Erle lit a cigarette. "How does it work out in practice? I mean—that's theory, of course, and the long hairs can say those things, but what does it actually mean to you and me?"

She looked at him from the corner of a liquid brown eye. "Would you believe it, I have been on this run for three hundred and twenty years?"

Erle stared at her—all over.

"Surely that isn't possible," he said finally.

She lifted her chin. "See any lines in my neck? And never an Osterhus in my whole life."

The champagne cocktails came, and Erle dropped a five-dollar gold piece into the change box. It rang a bell and his change clattered into it cup. The box said, "Thank you, sir."

"Let's drink to you," he said. "But you haven't told me your name."

"Zola. Sometimes they call me Zola Procyon, because I've been on this run so long."

"How long will it seem to us on board the ship?"

"About eight hours."

He raised his glass again. "Here's to Procyon."

For the first time he took a good look at her fingers. They did not look old. The skin was soft and velvety, but the digits clutched the glass as if they were straining at it.

"To Procyon's eleventh planet," she said, "A waterless world. And after this one, we can dance, if you'd like."

He heard a couple of Saturnians having a loud argument, and he noted that he himself felt lightheaded when he arose. Perhaps the peculiar physics accompanying this terrific acceleration did not require much alcohol to produce intoxication.

She started out, swinging a little on her tiptoes, and somehow the fact of her calendar age did not seem important, for she was a very lovely woman.

One of the Saturnians arose. He still wore rough clothing, and apparently had just come from the mines. The second miner surged up from his chair and lunged at the first one. They began to wrestle over the table. A glass of water teetered and then seemed to catapult toward Zola, with the water spraying out in a sheet.

Zola screamed. She stood on her tiptoes, rigid, and her fingertips dug into Erle's back. She didn't stop screaming until her face was black. Then she fell, limp and unconscious. A steward ran up.

"She'll be okay. A little water splashed on her. That's all."

Erle watched two men carry her away. He took a walk around the lounge. The Saturnians were apologizing to the steward.

"That's all right," the steward said, "You have to expect strange things on a ship like this. Eight hundred G's will throw many a good man out of sync."

"Give our apologies to the girl. We didn't mean to scare her."

"Don't worry about Zola. She's out of sync all the time. She was born that way. She's a hydrophoiac."

Erle lit a cigarette to cover his astonishment. He should have known something was wrong, for now he remembered the strain that was evident in Zola's fingers. But he hadn't paid much attention, and certainly he never would have linked it up with abnormal fear of water, although, come to think of it, the electronic waiter had not brought a glass of water for them.

Erle walked on to the great three-dimensional map of the Fourth Universe. The Sun was a tiny yellow pinpoint out toward the edge of the Second Metagalaxy, past Hercules. The Earth was completely invisible, but as he stood there he had no feeling of being so far away. He found the tiny golden arrow that marked the progress of the *Aleph Null* toward Procyon, just as a nasal voice said in his ear, "Small universe, ain't it, bud?"

Erle started and looked around. There was Jastrow, with his dead white skin and the red fringe of hair pasted on it.

"It sure is," said Erle.

"Like a drink?"

They sat down and Erle asked, "Are you going to Regulus with the show?"

"Not me," said Jastrow. "I've got my own show."

Erle did a little calculation involving a basic figure of ten cents a light-second. Then he said, "You must have done well in the system, to be going to Procyon."

Their drinks came, but Jastrow didn't even look at his. He threw a gold piece into the receiving box. "I've got an angel, bud—and you can have one too." His intense black eyes drilled into Erle's. "How would you like to make a cool million? Enough to buy anything on Earth a man could want."

Erle studied the man. "I wonder if money would make it possible for a man to get a job where he could do some useful work."

Jastrow looked suspicious. "You talkin' my language, bud?"

Erle killed his drink, "Have you ever been stared at by the chrono, by the day, by the week, by the year?"

Jastrow eyed him. "Maybe you need another one?"

"I'll buy one," said Erle, "but it isn't a drink I need. I like the carnival," said Erle. "I get a kick every time I look down the midway. But I'm a strong, healthy man. I want to make a living in a normal way. If I were handicapped, it would be different. But I'm not."

"You're a normal man in a neurotic world—what more of a handicap could you ask? You think a neurotic man is going to let you compete against him? How'd you get started anyway?"

"The scientists. I wouldn't know I was normal if it hadn't

been for them. They took me to conventions and meetings all over the world, and then The Man got hold of me."

"But how come the scientists had so much to say about you? Your parents shoulda' stopped it."

"Parents? I have no parents," He stared at Jastrow coldly.

"It must have been a pretty terrible accident for you not to have no parents."

"It was," said Erle. "A terrible accident."

Jastrow finished his drink and ordered a third, "What do you want to do most?"

"I'd like," Erle said earnestly, "to have some kind of work where I could produce, something with my hands. That, I think, is the ultimate test of a man's usefulness—his ability to produce something functional and important with his hands."

He saw then that Jastrow didn't know what he was talking about. Jastrow was probing him. For some reason, Jastrow was determined to get him in his show.

Erle looked far away, "I think I'd like to make machinery: clocks, automatic nose wipers, space ships."

Jastrow shoved the drink in front of Erle who now felt cold sober, "What do you say? Nobody can ignore a million bucks—not in these days when there's no income tax."

Erle looked at him. "It sounds good, but I'm under contract."

Jastrow looked as though he didn't feel Erle was sincere.

"What's a contract? They can't do anything to you for quitting."

"I don't break contracts," Erle said firmly.

CHAPTER SIX

ERLE SAW ZOLA about two hours later. Her olive-skinned face with its beautiful contours showed the strain of her terror, but she had changed to a yellow costume that brought out the red in her dusky thighs. She slipped into a magnetic field chair beside him and lay back, half-reclining, one knee drawn up.

"Sorry I messed things up for you," she said.

Erle's lids dropped a little as he looked her over, "I'm sorry, too," he said, and meant it.

"That awful water!" she moaned. "I thought I would die. We're about to commence deceleration, and I feel drowsy. You never said what you're doing out here."

"I'm with a freak show."

"You don't look like a freak."

"I'm perfectly normal."

She looked him over more carefully now. "Well, this is sure something," she said. "You're a freak because you're not a character."

Erle thought for a moment. "Would there be such a thing as a huge snake on board?"

"It would have been put on board at the Moon," he persisted. "Maybe it was listed as baggage."

"That's impossible. Baggage space is so precious that every ounce of cargo is rigorously inspected. Nothing like that could ever get by without its being known."

He thought of Jastrow. "What if somebody was bribed to keep silent?"

She shook her head. "Utterly impossible. Everything bigger than a mousetrap is X-rayed."

Jastrow had tried to hire him for a freak show, and that, he told himself, had implications. In the first place, the big snake was a natural in the Ninth Galaxy, even if you did have to pay half a billion dollars to transport a show to paying territory. But if Jastrow was carrying a show, where was the snake? Jastrow certainly wasn't depending on hiring his attraction on board the *Aleph Null.*

Why were the metagalactic officials spending

$6,200,000,000 to send him to Regulus? Why had Jastrow offered him a million dollars to break his contract?

The figures left him dizzy, and it was just as well. He wasn't getting anywhere anyway.

The *Aleph Null* had been big, but the *Infinity* was at least one mile long and quarter of a mile high. It in turn was like a mite attached to the tremendous plastic bubble that covered Terminal City on the airless and waterless eleventh planet of Procyon. It was a place of moving, colored walks, flashing arrows, millions of inhabitants and a constant stream of freight moving in all directions.

The *Infinity* was of the 62,000,000 class—meaning that she displaced 62,000,000 tons. She was equipped with electromagnetic circuits to counterbalance the effects of acceleration as well as those of gravitation, and she was big enough and complete enough for an inter-universe run if one should ever be established. The only factor that prevented that now, the steward said, was the lack of suitable energy.

Erle drew a deep breath and lit a cigarette. "What is this time-effect of the speed of light," he asked.

The steward connected a magnetic lounge chair. "I'll tell you how it has been explained to me. But you've got to remember I'm no scientist and I don't guarantee anything. When an object moves—anywhere, at any velocity—the atoms in it begin to slow down."

"At the kind of speeds you encounter on a planet, the slow down is too small to measure. But as your velocity approaches the speed of light it becomes noticeable—more and more so until at exactly light speed the atomic particles—principally the electrons—stand still. If the atoms that make up a human body slow down, your rate of living slows down. If the atoms go only half as fast, you live only half as fast. In an Earth year you would age only six months."

"Then at exactly light speed we wouldn't grow old at all."

"Theoretically we wouldn't. Actually it is impossible to travel at exactly that speed—but we can go over."

"Then what happens?"

"The spin of the particles is reversed, and you or anything traveling at that speed gets younger." He paused an instant, then went on, "They watch our light-second time very carefully—though it doesn't make a substantial difference unless you're traveling all the time. By the way, I noticed your card. You're normal, aren't you?"

"Yes—sometimes to my regret."

"You won't regret it this time. Come with me." The steward led Erle to the lounge, where a lovely blonde-haired girl was sitting alone. The steward spoke to her, "Miss Castiliano, Mr. Bertron."

She smiled gorgeously, "Won't you sit down?"

She wasn't standing up, but Erle thought she was rather tall for a girl—five feet ten anyway—with beautiful smooth legs of a creamy color that was deepened by pale green shorts.

"You and Miss Castiliano," the steward was saying, "have a great deal in common. You are both normal."

Erle, starting to sit down, looked sharply up at the steward, but he was moving away on the autowalk. Erle looked back at Miss Castiliano. "Two normals?" he asked incredulously.

She smiled. "Two normals."

He was looking into a pair of beautiful green eyes in a face of ivory surmounted by shining platinum blonde hair. The green eyes were smiling, and Erle started to light a cigarette. Then he thought better of it. "Won't you have a drink?"

She smiled. Her eyes had not left his. "If you wish."

Erle looked into the green eyes again. "So you're normal?"

Her "Yes" was musical.

"Did you," he asked, "once appear in a freak show as a

normal human?"

She seemed faintly amused. "Come to think of it, I did. And now that you mention it, that's where I was when somebody picked up my contract with the Venus Varieties."

"Did you know a Headless Woman?"

Miss Castiliano sipped her drink. Her fingernails were tinted pink. "I ran into her a couple of times—once out around Uranus, I think, and again on Jupiter."

"She said you broke a button loose at the Nine Planets."

She smiled, and every time she did that, it raised his blood pressure ten millimeters. "Maybe I did," she said, "but the binge was deliberate. I got tired of being stared at by a bunch of neurotics who didn't know enough to come in out of the sawdust."

He finished his drink. "I've felt like that," he admitted, "but this is the first time I've heard it in words."

"I know about you," she said. "You've been the blow-off for Greater Galactic for years. I very nearly looked you up when I was in the same town, but thought maybe you'd be a fussy little baldheaded man with glasses and false teeth, and I decided not to risk it." She studied him as she finished her drink; "I was a fool," she said.

He looked at her and took a deep breath. "We're still young," he said, "or have you been rejuvenated about six times?"

"Not me. I'm exactly what you see."

"What I see is lovely."

"My first name is Naomi."

"It sounds nice. What happened when you lost your place in the show?"

"As soon as I got my persecution complex diagnosis, I went out for a job. But naturally nobody trusted me. The neurotics were afraid to have me around. The men were afraid of losing their jobs, and the women were afraid of losing their husbands—everybody defending what little they've got under the laws of society. That seems to be the only strength most of them have."

He paid for the drinks. "Have you seen any freaks on this trips?"

"Not a one," she said slowly.

He thought about it. "Do we have anything in common besides normality?"

"I have absolute pitch."

"And I have absolute motion." She began to look worried. "It doesn't seem to me that they bought our contracts because we're freaks."

"What do you suppose they want us for then?" she asked.

"I don't know," he said. He looked into her green eyes and took a deep breath.

THE BYRD snuggled down in the cozy warmth of Erle Bertron's mind. There has been nothing like this for a good long time, and if he was lucky he wouldn't have to move again for a couple of hundred years.

The lights were dim. Erle was in his bed but he couldn't sleep. With his eyes wide open in the dark, he kept seeing Miss Castiliano's soft green eyes. She could talk, but she didn't talk all the time. She was normal and so was he.

He wondered if he should tell her the full truth about himself. He'd wait until they knew each other better. He wished the trip to Regulus would last for ten years instead of eight days. He got up and wandered into the lounge. Two humanoids were standing before the big map, apparently exchanging thoughts, for, although no word was spoken, occasionally one would nod or shake his head. Mind reading was not uncommon in some parts of the galaxy.

Eric walked slowly around the big room. The menus were still illuminated, but the hidden lights were dimmed. Erle sat at the table which he and Naomi had occupied that afternoon. For the first time he noticed there were brilliantly colored macaws—red, yellow, and blue—in the treetops. But the birds were quiet, and the wall of the lounge was a transparent sheet of something that formed one side of an aquarium.

As he watched, a small, brown squid shot up from the depths, fouling the water with an inky discharge, and wrapped its two club-like tentacles around a filmy, almost transparent tropical fish that had been sleepily fanning the water with a long blue tail. The squid reversed itself and shot back to the bottom. The inkiness slowly cleared away, but the small blue fish was gone, and down among the rocks an expanding cloud of mud arose from the movements of the squid.

It was like a bad dream, and Erle shook his head. Then something dropped over him from behind, and he was pulled backward. He tried to free himself by thrashing and kicking, but his movements were not effectual. He had one glimpse of the two humanoids at the map, but they didn't look his way. He seemed to be in a tunnel, pulled backward rapidly and soundlessly. It was like being sucked into a vacuum. Then he was brought up hard against some sort of cushion, and sent sprawling.

A lisping voice said something in no solar language that he had ever heard, and almost simultaneously he felt that intolerable tightening and prickling of the nerves which accompanies sounds of ultrasonic frequency. The sensation was followed by the goose pimple noise of a fingernail scraping glass. Finally a command came to his mind—not in words but in abstract thought.

"Get to your feet and follow the light."

He was sitting on the floor. A small green glow appeared in the darkness, and he walked toward it almost automatically. The rustling and scraping continued at his side. Finally the command, "Stop," took form in his mind.

The rustling went ahead. Then suddenly lights blazed all about him. At first he thought he was in a room filled with brown gas, but this clarified. He breathed deeply and was relieved to feel air going into his lungs. He thought he detected the odor of bromine.

An image began to resolve itself before him—the upthrust head of a snake with black velvet scales on its back. He felt that brain-sucking power in his mind, and pulled his eyes away with an effort.

He saw Jastrow.

"What vicious trick is this?" Erle demanded. "You didn't bring that snake on board with you."

The great reptile's vertical eyes seemed to grow larger and larger, closer and closer. But somehow Erle managed to resist the deadly menace of the thing.

"Hypnotism is no good," he heard Jastrow say. "He can't do it when he's hypnotized."

"Do what?" Erle tried to ask, but his voice made no sound.

Something flowed between the snake and Jastrow then. It probably was thought, but it was much too fast for Erle to follow. He squared away at them both, but before he could make his anger felt the snake's forked tongue ran out farther than usual, and a sharp, searing flame touched his nerves. It flashed through his body. It was like a dart of white fire. And when it vanished he found himself on his toes, his body stretched taut.

"Those high-frequency sonics are a little painful sometimes," the snake said. "You will see that we have ways of persuasion. You will note that they leave no visible mark. You could very easily go out of here broken and shattered in mind. But you would have no evidence against us. You would merely be a supposedly normal Earthman who has suddenly turned neurotic."

Erle said finally, "Who is Jastrow?"

The snake's countenance did not change. "He is one of my associates."

Jastrow said, "Are we going to make him work with us?"

"I think so," the snake said. "But of course it must be done delicately. There must be no marks of violence or evidence of any kind."

"That eliminates dismemberment," Jastrow said, and a chill went down Erle's back.

"It also eliminates anything that might destroy his ability to cooperate with us."

The snake turned a little, and seemed to concentrate. For a moment Erle felt nothing. Then, slowly, he began to sweat. It was an odd kind of heat that seemed to come from inside of his bones and radiate out through his flesh. It was like a burning flame in the marrow of his bones.

"Infra-red," said Jastrow. "You like it?"

For a blessed moment Erle blacked out. Then the fire raced along his nerves again and brought him up from the floor. His hands were shaking uncontrollably. He tried to hold his head firm while he looked at the snake. He said hoarsely, "You will gain nothing by torturing me. You've got to have my willing consent or you won't accomplish anything."

The snake's words formed in his mind, "We shall see."

Again the heat began to pour into his blood, like a hand with a thousand steel fingers, probing every corner of his mind. So unbearable was the torment that he cried out in agony and lunged at the snake's eyes.

He might as well have hurled himself against a flat steel wall, for his hands could find nothing to take hold of. It could only mean that the snake's body was not in its real body. The scales were not chitin but some kind of metal. It seemed probable that Jastrow, too, had an artificial body that he could cast off at will.

A sonic discharge struck him and knocked him down. He got up and swayed helplessly. The sonic projection came again, a tremendous jolt, and he went down flat on his face. The sonic discharges came with a frequency of about one per millichron.

Erle remained prone, physically helpless, with the snake probing at his brain. Through all his torture he knew they did not want to kill him, and that knowledge stiffened his resistance. From somewhere deep within him, from the ataxic layers of his brain, came a strength that seemed to go beyond the merely physical. He drew it up from wherever it was stored, and he used it against them. It enabled him to resist the cruel, relentless probing. The agony continued but it had no power to bend him to its will. Dully he wondered if they would keep it up forever. He wondered if he would be sane when they got through with him.

Erle realized finally that he was alone. Jastrow and the snake had vanished and he was lying on a glass floor, about which lingered the faint odor of bromine. He lay there for a while, afraid to move for fear that the slightest physical effort would bring back the hurt.

Then he heard Naomi's voice, raised in concern, "It was this way, I'm sure!" He managed to roll over on his back. Footsteps were approaching and he could detect the voices of men, too, and the clicking of metal instruments. He was trying to rise when they found him a few seconds later.

He looked up at Naomi. His throat and mouth were so parched that he was unable to speak. Naomi screamed when she saw him. Two men in white uniforms approached, and helped him to his feet. Erle looked at Naomi and tried to smile, but she was blurred in his sight and seemed to be swinging back and forth like a pendulum. The heat was leaving his bones, but the instant he moved again an agonizing pain half doubled him up.

"Get him to a doctor," Naomi whispered urgently, "Hurry."

"Looks like an epileptic attack to me," said one of the men in White.

"It couldn't be," Naomi said indignantly, "He's normal."

"It isn't anything to be ashamed of."

"I didn't say it was...but Mr. Bertron is normal I tell you."

IT WAS LIKE heaven to lie on the doctor's magnetic couch, although the tapping finger made him want to scream.

"You're badly dehydrated. Had a fever?"

"Not a normal fever. It was something much worse—"

The doctor was looking at his chart. "Had many of these attacks before?"

Erle tightened his lips and said nothing.

The doctor brushed aside his failure to answer. "I see you're rated normal."

"Yes."

"Quite a phenomenon, eh? Well, this is perhaps a little atavistic throwback to some deep-seated neuroticism that hasn't appeared before. Suppose I give you a sedative and you come back tomorrow for a checkup."

Erle figured there was only one thing to check on—the nature of his tormentors inside their disguises. But that might prove a very difficult task.

Naomi was waiting outside for him, and she was like a fresh breeze from the ocean. He kissed her, impulsively, and for a moment the wonder of her so close to him blotted out everything else. Then, gradually, he became aware that she was talking to him in an earnest, solicitous voice.

"I missed you yesterday and then I began to hear that strange sound at about forty-one thousand vibrations per second. You know I have absolute pitch?"

"Yes."

"I told the steward about the sound, but he insinuated I was neurotic," Her green eyes flashed.

"I argued the sound indicated something unusual, but nobody else could hear it because of the high frequency."

"Don't they have sonic detectors?"

"That's what I asked, but they put me off. Of course normal human ears seldom hear over twenty thousand vibrations."

"I'm glad it was you who heard it," Erle said.

"All this was yesterday. I made so much fuss that the steward got two assistants and went with me. I traced it to where we found you."

"You probably saved my life—if not my sanity. But isn't it miraculous that you, who are probably one out of millions with supersonic hearing, was on board?"

"I think," she said, "it's miraculous that we are both on board together." She frowned a little. "Aren't those goose bumps on your arms?"

He nodded. "You're pretty when you frown, but you're beautiful when you smile. Let's see you be beautiful."

At last the Byrd could turn over and settle down. Those damned Alphirkians, in their fantastic disguises! For a while the Byrd had been tempted to take a hand, but it had gotten along very nicely for quite a while on its cardinal principle of minding its own business. Erle Bertron had survived and in addition had learned something that eventually would be of value to the metagalaxy, with no interference from the Byrd.

CHAPTER SEVEN

ERLE FINISHED THE trip to Regulus in a sort of golden haze, from which now and then appeared a pair of eyes, sea green and sea deep, that looked long and questioningly into his.

They were two normal persons neither of whom had ever before talked to a normal person. Besides, they were both perfect physical specimens, and the result was something like the force that holds the atomic nucleus together.

The steward cleared his throat with considerable violence, "I guess you two didn't hear the warning bell."

Naomi, dawdling over a Metagalactic fizz, smiled at the steward. Erle said, "I guess not." Then he straightened. "Did you say warning bell?"

"Yes, we've been picked up by the tractor ray, and we will be down in eight or ten chronos, but it probably will take you most of the day to get cleared." Erle was worried when he turned to Naomi. "Here we're both going to be in Regulus City, which has a population of eight or ten billion, and we both have different addresses, and now when we've just become acquainted we'll have to separate. How can we find each other again?"

"We'll be back on Earth eventually," Naomi said. "Suppose we both get in touch with Greater Galactic."

"It may be a long time. What do you suppose they want us for in Regulus City?"

She shook her platinum blond head. "I don't know. There aren't any other freaks—unless they are from other planets. And the strange thing is that you and I aren't really freaks. Don't tell me the metagalactic officials don't know that!"

"I'm sure they do," He put his diagnosis card back in his paper-thin billfold.

"Maybe some metagalactic anthropologist is preparing an encyclopedia of life forms in the universe, and we're going to be examples of humans. It's distinctly possible, you know."

A glowing violet light appeared in the ceiling, "I guess that means we've landed," said Erle.

She stood up, tall and slim and incredibly beautiful.

"We might as well go down together," Erle said.

"Okay, Mr. Normal Male." She took his arm.

He paused for an instant. Other Earth-people were hurrying past them on both sides, but Erle stopped her. "Just say the word and I'll buy you a mountain with a big yellow moon."

Amusement tinkled in Naomi's voice, "Are you trying to high pressure me?"

"We'll have to go," he said softly.

They took the autowalk to the elevator. It was crowded, and she had to turn sidewise to him. "Think," she whispered. "The Solar System was so big we never made the same show. Earth was so big we were only in the same town once. But out here on Regulus, two hundred light-years from home, we found each other just like *that*." She snapped her fingers.

He smiled down at her. "It's a small universe, isn't it?"

There was a great ramp sloping down. Naomi swayed and covered her mouth with her slim white fingers, "Fire!" she exclaimed, "The world's on fire!"

Erle stared at the walls of the great dome they had entered. This was larger than the one on Procyon, and in every direction without a break was a solid bank of blue flames. Fire—twisting, turning, writhing, sweeping in great loops and masses of leaping flames. It was blue, and there was no break in it. Like water, it churned and swirled, and they seemed immersed in it.

Erle looked at Naomi's white face and back at the tremendous pressure of the fire. "We landed on a sun," he said slowly, "A blue star—the double or triple companion of Regulus. Probably a small star—but a hot one. Blue indicates a surface temperature of around twenty thousand degrees Centigrade."

"But why?"

"Probably for safety. What kind of being could come through this heat without a lot of preparation?"

"The dome must be a perfect insulator."

"Either that, or they use the heat for refrigeration."

"Isn't a sun a ball of gas? How would they anchor a city here?"

"A servo-controlled balance among gravity, centrifugal force, and the pressure of the burning gas."

Naomi shuddered. "What if something went wrong—just for an instant?"

A voice came from a loud speaker, "Earth people will please present their papers at the Blue Window."

They got in line. Naomi put her papers on the glass counter. They were stamped in strange characters and pushed back to her, along with a graceful pair of glass shoes. "You will please take the yellow lane and follow the directions given you by the shoes. As long as you use these, you cannot be lost in the city."

Naomi stood for a moment, waiting for Erle to get his papers stamped. He also received a pair of directional shoes. "You will take the pink lane, Mr. Bertron."

Erle turned out of the line and stopped beside Naomi.

"I'm frightened," she said, and tried to laugh. "It's so far from home."

"There's nothing to be afraid of," he assured her. "Let's get our jobs finished, and then we'll get in touch through Greater Galactic if there is no other way. In the meantime, I'll get in touch with you the first minute I can. Only—I'm dubious. They seem to run things their own way out here."

The sea-green eyes looked into his. "All right," she said. She turned and went through the yellow gate and got on the autowalk. She waved once and was gone.

Erle could see Naomi no longer. He found the pink gate and stepped on the walk.

Regulus City was a great sphere of life, motion, and activity. On every side it stretched beyond the limit of his eyesight, and both above and below were innumerable levels, with moving walks—narrow ones for people, wide ones for freight, slow ones and fast ones—walks of all colors curving to left and right and up and down. It was a vast maze of motion, in which color was the only universal language. What, Erle wondered, would they do with a person whose eyes were sensitive only to ultraviolet?

The pink lane began to slant downward, and the blue fire became no longer visible. He was deep inside the city. Presently he approached a crosswalk, and a voice from his shoes said, "Mr. Bertron, you will please take the green walk to your right."

He changed. The green walk descended more rapidly. Its speed, he estimated, was about half the speed of a sun-powered autocar on the elevated cross-continent highways of Earth. The many lights around him began to blur. Down, down, while he wondered where Naomi was and when they would both get back to Earth. And—he had to admit it—even neurotic Earth sounded good to him now.

The next day he was delivered into a small room that gave a first impression of being alive, for waving bands of pastel colors arose from the floor and pursued one another up the walls to a black ceiling that showed the twinkling lights of the Milky Way.

This room was singularly bare of furnishings. A lounge of some strange material faced a plain flat table that seemed to have no legs, but was projected from the wall. Beyond these items, however, the room was filled with a vitality of thoughts and feelings almost substantial enough to touch.

Erle stopped. Above the small table was the same purple ball that had come into the sideshow of Greater Galactic. It was as he remembered it—about two feet in diameter, topped with a tiny aerial, and on its front the diamond-incrusted insignia of the banded heavens.

Strange-sounding words came from the aerial. "Please sit down, Mr. Bertron. Make yourself comfortable on the lounge."

Erle stared at the fabulous designation of the metagalaxy.

When he had first seen the purple ball in the carnival tent, he had experienced great excitement, for he had felt himself to be in an awesome presence, but now as he faced that presence in Regulus City, the truth dawned upon him with overwhelming clarity.

He was in the *headquarters* of the intergalactic system!

He had been compulsively summoned and had traveled a great many light-years for one purpose only—to stand in this room and talk face to face with the august ruler of the metagalaxy.

This was no ordinary encounter. It was breath taking and awe-inspiring, and it was made more so by the very power and dignity with which the atmosphere was charged.

He needed to sit down when he was invited to do so. He was weak with the realization that he was in the actual presence of the being whose will was law throughout the entire metagalaxy.

"Sit down, Erle," the invitation came again.

For a moment Erle stared, still hardly believing. Then he looked behind him.

"Anywhere," said the purple ball. "The currents will find you."

Erle tried it—gingerly—and felt resistance. He let his muscles relax and sat back.

The purple ball descended several feet—apparently to be on a level with his head. It floated there while the voice said, "Before I came here I was a line officer in the metagalactic space fleet. If you will think of me as such, I'm quite sure you'll feel more at ease."

"Very well, sir, I'll confess that…all of this has shaken me up a bit. Perhaps 'unnerved' would be as good a word as any."

"Make yourself comfortable. I have a story to tell you. It is important to the metagalaxy, perhaps to the Fourth Universe. Undoubtedly you have realized by this time that you are not here as a freak, and I assume you have been puzzled as to what other reason might be responsible for this long and expensive trip."

Each word had an earnest ring.

Erle nodded, deciding that he had perhaps already said too much.

The purple ball paused, then went on quickly, "You might have been told before, but I felt it better for you not to know."

Erle thought of his tortured hours with Jastrow and the 'snake,' and said, "I think you were right."

If the general was aware of his thoughts he gave no sign, "The metagalaxy is up against an age-old problem—one that has vexed universes, galaxies, and planets since the Beginning. That is the need for power."

Erle looked startled. "Power? I thought—"

"Take power at a planetary level. In Earth's past you have depended on such primitive energy sources as coal, oil, wood, uranium. Such sources have been extremely expensive."

"We use sun power now."

"In your history, as in the history of every planet, there have been many crises over the lack of energy. Sources have been there, but they have required inordinate expenditure of human energy to transform them into mechanical energy. Isn't it true that whole populations have died of starvation for lack of cheap transportation? One part of your Earth would have a surplus of food, while other parts would have none—and there was no one with authority or energy available to distribute these foods and make them equally available to all."

"Not within my time."

"Possibly not," the general conceded. "Now you are drawing on sun power. But when the radiating force of the Sun begins to dwindle, what then?"

"That will be several billion years," Erle said and looked up at the ceiling.

"The universe is heading steadily toward entropy—a running down of all energy everywhere. Some call it chaos, some call it perfect order. It makes no difference, for the result is the same. All the atoms of the universe will be perfectly distributed in such a fashion that we shall not be able to extract more energy from any of them."

"I didn't realize power was so important."

"Energy is the great theme of the universe. Without energy, there will be no life, no stars, no movement of any kind—nothing but a cool glow from the entire universe. There will be nothing solid, for all atoms will be perfectly distributed."

I should imagine it would be a pretty big job to find energy for the whole universe."

"Yes—but not hopeless, as you will see. In the meantime, some citizens of the Second Metagalaxy are taking advantage of this lack of energy to win political power."

"You mean a cold war?"

The tiny aerial seemed to nod, "Incredible as it may seem, the directorship of the metagalaxy is engaged in a silent struggle with the Forty-third Galaxy of Alphirk. The Forty-third is spending vast amounts of energy to make other planets and galaxies dependent on them, and when the time is suitable they will come out in the open. If such a time comes, we shall find them in control of most of the energy sources, and we shall be compelled to accept their terms. This very city, for instance, requires a use of energy that to us now seems extravagant, since the Second Law of Thermodynamics appears to operate implacably.

"Matter is constantly being turned into energy, which is being squandered as radiation—radiation which for the most part we are powerless to convert into energy. The law also says that the equation is irreversible—that energy cannot be re-converted into matter. Pursued to its ultimate, that means that eventually there will be no matter, hence no life and no universe."

"And the metagalaxy is trying to do something about that?"

"We have always planned on the vastest imaginable scale, but now our plans are of little value. The Alphirkians, not interested in the distant future, are making every effort to upset the economy of the metagalaxy by getting control of the comparatively meager supplies of energy that remain."

Erle was still puzzled, "But on Earth we use water power," he said. "Water falls toward the sea, and turns a wheel that generates electricity."

"What gets the water to a place above the generator?" the general asked.

"Rain, I suppose."

"And what makes rain possible?"

"Well—sunlight."

"Exactly. Energy in the form of radiation from the sun. When the sun cools, there will be no more rain on Earth, and you will have no more water power, no more electricity, no more sun power."

"It begins to look as if the Alphirkians are wasting the energy resources of the universe."

"That's the tragic part of it. This reckless use of energy has to come to an end. Before it does, I think we may assume that the Alphirkians will take over the metagalactic government—and I think we are safe in saying their motives are not altruistic. Nothing we know about them points in that direction."

The purple ball seemed to look up, "Have you ever seen metagalactic war? It's an incredible waste of energy. Fleets of ships gasefied in an instant, worlds blown apart, stars turned into supernovae, trillions of life forms wiped out."

The voice lowered. "I have seen metagalactic war. I was present at the great battle about the year eighty-five thousand, when Frode Rockman, the only Earthman ever to attain metagalactic rank, beat off the invasion fleet of Mondobex and his insect hordes from the Greater Magellanic Cloud. I saw a battle fought over an area as big as a galaxy. I saw the lower heavens lighted up by the most furious blaze of radiation ever exhibited in the Fourth Universe. All that energy was lost forever—energy that would go far toward supplying the shortages that now exist."

Erle was silent.

"I have talked at length because I want you to know the situation. Your good will is necessary if you are to be of value to us."

"I don't quite see—"

"I want you to know that if the Alphirkians do try to take over, we shall have another metagalactic war, and a tremendous amount of energy will again be lost. War will mean nothing but fewer privileges for those already underprivileged."

"Do you care," asked Erle, "who actually runs the metagalaxy?"

"We have asked ourselves that question many times." Remiggon paused. "The answer is that we are willing for anyone to control the metagalaxy who will control it un-selfishly."

Suddenly Remiggon sounded tired. "There is only a certain amount of energy available in the universe. When that is gone, no matter who is in control, we shall have entropy. In other words, when war comes, that in itself will be an indication that the Alphirkians are running out of energy. It is a very vital problem, for energy is the theme of the universe."

He paused once more, very briefly this time, and then went on. "We have developed the hyperdrive, the solar drive, the ultra-drive, the sixth-dimension Schweickhard drive, the pluperfect vacuum impulsive thrust—I could go on for days."

Erle said soberly, "Yes, sir."

"In short," said the general, "here we can do anything but make energy out of stray radiation. It is more tragic because we are not a run-down universe. The Fourth is young compared to the incredibly ancient Second that lies below Achernar. Nevertheless, our energy requirements are far greater than our supply. I am told that other metagalaxies do not have this problem, that it must be due to some terrific driving force that has centered on us."

Erle was staring at the purple ball. Abruptly it revolved, and he knew the general was looking at him. "You are wondering about me," the general said, "and I will tell you, if you could open this ball—which would be something of a project, for we are practically indestructible—you would find a few whiffs of odorless, colorless gas. Yet that gas thinks and talks. It has emotions. It plans and it worries. It has a great deal of knowledge and experience, but it is not all-powerful. That is why you are here, Erle Bertron. We believe you maybe able to do something we cannot do."

Erle said with a slight tremor in his voice, "I don't see how."

Remiggon looked at him for a moment, as if speculating, and then said, "Follow me."

CHAPTER EIGHT

ON AN AUTOWALK they traveled through the laboratory, kilometer after kilometer. Occasionally they came up to invisible, reflection-less glass walls, apparently keyed to the general's voice, for after a few words that sounded to Erle like, "Cucumber, cucumber, strawberries and gravy," a section would slide up and allow them to go through.

Finally the general stopped before a white porcelain door, "This is the conference," he said, "the governing body of the Second Metagalaxy. Don't be alarmed."

He nodded reassuringly.

The door dissolved. The general floated through, and Erle followed. They stopped, and suddenly around them, as if they had formed from the air, floated half a dozen purple balls and sat half a dozen humanoids—the fabulous metagalactic conference, the most powerful governing body in the universe of stars.

The general was speaking, "Gentlemen...I have Erle Bertron with me."

"He has the gift of absolute motion?" asked a silkily rustling voice.

"He is said to have it," the general answered, "As I reported in my neutrogram, I did not think it advisable to call attention by testing him. I do not vouch for his gift. I merely say that he is ready for testing."

A heavy, impatient voice came from the transmuter of a Regulian. "Let's find out."

"Will the engineers expand the room?"

There was a whispering sound as the walls of the chamber receded. The ceiling went up out of sight, and the floor around them shrank away, leaving the conference sitting on a small circle of floor in the center of a very large globular area.

A humanoid buckled a strap around Erle's neck and suspended on his chest an instrument panel that held dials and lights and gauges.

"Now," said the Regulian with the heavy voice, "you will press the red button and float to the center of this sphere. We are considerably below the center, so you will ascend. Are you ready?"

Erle took a deep breath. "Yes, sir. I am ready."

Erle was braced for a shock, but it didn't come. He just quietly floated up until he was three or four thousand feet above them. There he stopped—with nothing tangible to hold onto.

"You won't fall," said the general's voice from one of the instruments on his chest. "Don't be afraid to move."

Erle took another deep breath.

"Now," the heavy voice said, "the panel is a relay for power to move you for a short distance. Also there is a very sensitive encephalo-pickup and amplifying device. If you can 'tune in' to absolute motion, the device will transfer your conscious or instinctive knowledge into physical reality.

"In other words, when you reach the conclusion that you are in tune, your body will be locked in that relationship and you will remain at absolute rest while your surroundings here will demonstrate the rotation and revolution, drift, and any erratic movements, such as nutation, precession, and so on— whether of the star, the galaxy, the metagalaxy, or the universe itself. Do you understand all that?"

"Yes. My body will stay parallel with the seat of absolute motion and will travel in its same direction at the same velocity."

"Very good—except for the velocity. Since the velocity may be considerable, perhaps even approximating the speed of light, and since our space here is limited, we are going to start with an extremely low power—about one millionth of the energy potential necessary to duplicate actual velocities. Also you will be stopped automatically if there is danger. All set?"

"I'm set," said Erle. He hoped this would not fail, but he had no way of knowing. The scientists on Earth had checked him, but their verdict had been based on microscopic evidence, and, now that he was in a spot where so much depended on it, he was scared.

The lights suddenly went out. Erle was suspended in total blackness, his temples throbbing.

"The power is on. When you have decided the direction and velocity of absolute motion, your decision will be, translated into movement. Go ahead."

Erle tightened his lips. He closed his eyes against the dark and began to concentrate. At first he saw Naomi with her platinum hair and her sea-green eyes, but he had to put her out of his mind. He began to relax, and then he felt it coming—a sort of mental convolution that always made him think of folding his mind in against himself, and blocking out everything except one vital perception—that of motion, absolute motion—motion that came to him from a tremendous distance.

He felt himself go into a semi-trance, and that, he knew, was right. With his mind he began to reach, to grope in the dark, not looking for a movement of things but a movement of forces. He began to feel the nearness of the vital perception—as a man sometimes knows he is about to walk into a wall in the dark. It came closer until it was almost tangible, until it felt like air currents flowing around him in the blackness.

He had now lost all sense of direction. There was no feeling of standing up or of lying down. He tested the currents of force with his mind. They were the force he had always felt. He relaxed still further, and let his mind go with the force. Abruptly the currents no longer flowed around him, and he knew he was moving with them.

This seemed to go on for a long time, like a pleasant, dreamless sleep. Then abruptly the lights came on.

Erle looked down. The tiny circular floor that held the metagalactic conference was no longer beneath him.

"Very good, Mr. Bertron. Are you ready to try it again?"

"Yes. I'm ready," He wanted to know if they had been able to tell anything, if they were hopeful or disappointed. But he could tell nothing from the toneless voice, and he did not ask.

He found himself floating upward to his left and to his rear. He reached the level of the conference and passed it, going on up to what must have been his former position.

"The coordinates are the same," said the general. The lights went out. He felt himself spun about and then tumbled. "At your leisure, Mr. Bertron."

Erle stretched out and closed his eyes again. This time the force-currents came faster. He swung into them, took hold of them, and floated with them. He seemed to move faster.

Again the lights went up. Again he was below the conference. Again he floated back into position.

On the ninth try he failed. "I'm tired," he said.

"Understandable," said the general.

Erle floated back to the center of the circular floor. A long roll of graph paper was on the desk in front of the purple ball with the heavy voice. "You may be pleased to know our observations indicate that you are aligning yourself with the same motion every time. Your velocity and direction were identical and constant. Whether your alignment is with the absolute motion that we seek, we cannot know until the engineers have thoroughly checked the graphs."

They began to talk among themselves, in sounds that obviously did not have their origin in any human throat.

Presently the question was asked Erle, "Can you repeat this demonstration tomorrow, Mr. Bertron?"

"I think so."

"You will be conducted to your quarters by General Remiggon, and I hope you will not take this amiss—you will be well guarded, Mr. Bertron. You have become potentially the most valuable property in the Second Metagalaxy."

Erle hesitated, "It might be something else I'm tuning in on."

"Don't worry about that, Mr. Bertron. Our engineers will find out."

"But I'm normal."

The general chuckled. "It is one of the delightful idiocies of Earth civilization that it is commonly thought the great gifts of talent are given only to neurotics. It was an idea started by the neurotics themselves, and fostered by others who did not understand talents that were beyond them. But I can tell you this: the very finest talent discoverable is a normal entity. Give him intelligence and drive, and you have a combination that no neurotic can hope to equal. Now let's have no more nonsense."

The purple ball revolved from side to side as if the general was shaking his head. "You do your job. Let us decide how good a job it is."

The walls closed in, the floor came up, the ceiling descended. Erle followed the general to his quarters. "It is a little miraculous," the general said, "that a normal person like you could have developed on such a strange planet as Earth."

Erle made no comment.

Half a dozen purple balls waited outside. The general indicated them. "They have a rather astonishing set of perceptive faculties and an unusual, assortment of weapons. I doubt that any harm can come to you as long as you are in this city."

Erle asked one question, "Do you have reason to believe that anyone knows why I am here?"

The general evaded, "Regulus City is filled with entities from the entire metagalaxy. Some of them have unusual powers—and we do not want to take a chance. By the way, you will be staying with Admiral Blomberg."

So if the Regulians knew about the two who had appeared to him as Jastrow and the snake, and who had tortured him for two days, they were not saying. Erle wondered. The snake and Jastrow were not in their right forms, so he wouldn't recognize them when he met them. One of them might even be on the metagalactic conference. Remiggon himself—who knew?

SHE SCARED HIM—this Marissa, Admiral Blomberg's wife. She constantly watched him with the air of having found someone she adored...

"It's getting easier," Erle said after the sixth day of tests.

The heavy-voiced Regulian seemed almost to have a smile in his voice. "That is what we have been waiting to hear. Our astronomers believe that you do have absolute motion—though we have tried everything possible to confuse you. We have tilted this room. We have revolved it at a fantastic speed and we have even turned it upside down, but you have always moved in the same direction and at the same velocity."

General Remiggon told him to go back to his quarters and await their call...

Blomberg and Erle got out of sound of the tri-di, much to Marissa's disgust, and talked things over. Finally, one day, a message came from Remiggon for them both to appear at metagalactic headquarters.

The purple ball seemed filled with confidence. "You will both be glad to know," said the odd voice from the aerial, "that our astrodynamicists have concluded that Mr. Bertron does indeed have a sense of absolute motion. Naturally you know, Mr. Bertron, that we want to use that sense. It is a very rare gift, and it is quite possible that you are the only individual in the universe who has it."

"I will do everything I can," said Erle.

"One thing puzzles me," the general confessed. "I had expected the Alphirkians to make some move in your direction before this time, but your guards report no indication of it."

"What does an Alphirkian look like?" asked Erle.

"We are not sure. They are a secretive race and they have the ability to assume a great variety of disguises."

"You've had intelligence men in there?"

"Strangely enough, no. Their work is all done by androids—similar to robots but more humanoid in structure. These androids act as personal servants for the Alphirkians, and so far it has been impossible to get an agent close enough to find out what the Alphirkians are like. We know quite a bit about their operations. But we still have no information about them personally."

He decided to reveal what he knew. "I was kidnapped and tortured on the *Infinity* by a humanoid and a giant snake."

The general was quite still for an instant. Then he said sharply, "Were these the two who were next to your tent in Greater Galactic?"

"Yes."

The general sighed, "I'm afraid they evaded us. I was advised that those two were suspected of being Alphirkian, but they had done nothing and so we could not examine them. But now you say they were on the *Infinity*?"

"Yes."

Erle could imagine the general was frowning. "We have trouble keeping up with them. They must have embarked as two humanoids and later changed to the snake disguise."

The general sank to the level of the desk. "Two Alphirkians made up as humanoids left Regulus City yesterday shortly after I received a final report on your tests. I do not think that happened by chance."

"What will be their next move?" asked Admiral Blomberg.

"I'm not sure. It would seem they know about the tests— but do they have an engine that can turn the sense of absolute motion into power?"

"It wouldn't make any difference," Blomberg pointed out, "To them the most important thing is keeping this energy from the metagalaxy."

The purple ball rose abruptly. "We're fools," he said. "If they know about Erle, they know about the *Drifter*. All they have to do is wait for Erle to get on board. They then can capture the *Drifter* with Erle and the engine too."

"Speed of escape!" exclaimed Blomberg.

"Very well." The general was business-like again. "Takeoff time for the *Drifter* is set for six days from now. Watch your step, both of you. Be ready to move, Admiral. It will be better for you and your wife to go along, since you are from Erle's planet."

"Yes, sir."

"Meantime, Erle, you will continue to stay at the admiral's apartment."

ON THE SECOND day the admiral left early in the morning. Erle slept late, as he had done at the carnival. Then the visicom buzzed, and Blomberg's round face with the calm blue eyes appeared.

"Can you get to General Remiggon's headquarters right away—and bring Marissa?"

Erle sensed the urgency in his voice. "Right away, sir," he said.

Marissa was quite gay as they went up from the 110th

level. "It's the first time anything has happened around here," she said. Later, she waited in the reception room while Erle and the admiral went in General Remiggon's office.

"We have made arrangements," the general said, "for the test ship to leave in exactly fourteen chronos."

"I thought—" began Erle, but he caught Blomberg's eyes on him and didn't finish.

"There will be no opportunity to pack. You will all leave at once for Air lock fifty-eight. The guides will escort you to the gate. The mother ship is the *Nucleonic*, a scout carrier," The ball rose higher. "You will find Yjul, the inventor of the absolute-motion engine, and his wife, Fyllath, and your test pilot, Ekno, already on board."

The general suddenly disappeared. Then his voice came from a distance. "You will please take the green lane to Pier fifty-eight at once."

Blomberg got up and nodded at Erle. "That sounded like an order."

They went out through the reception room. Erle caught the general's voice faintly saying, "Good luck."

CHAPTER NINE

UNDER HEAVY GUARD, they went into the mother ship. The guards left, and then they entered the test ship. Yjul and Fyllath quietly introduced themselves, and Yjul said, "There is one member of the ship's company whom you have met, Mr. Bertron."

Erle followed him. Marissa walked closely at his side, her hand under his arm. There was unmistakable warmth and admiration in her eyes, and her manner was proprietary. The admiral walked ahead of them.

Yjul's leafy arms rustled as he led the way to a dark corner at one side of the control room, and Erle stared at the blonde hair and sea-green eyes of Naomi Castiliano.

"Naomi!" He started forward happily, but her unfriendly eyes held him back, and he was suddenly uncomfortably aware of Marissa beside him.

"Oh, you know each other," Marissa said, "How nice." Her eyes hardly noticed Naomi, she was so intent on keeping them on Erle.

"It's so good to see you," Erle said.

Naomi looked slantwise at Marissa, "I trust your stay in Regulus City has been pleasant," she answered, her voice coldly polite.

"Oh, yes—well—" He introduced the two women and was careful to emphasize that Marissa was Mrs. Blomberg, but for some reason this information seemed only to deepen the scorn in Naomi's flashing eyes.

"I suggest, dear," said the admiral, "that you and I go to look over the ship while Erle and Miss Castiliano renew their friendship."

"I'm sure there will be plenty of time for that later," said Marissa. "Why don't we all inspect the ship. You want to see it, don't you Erle?"

"Well, I—" He looked at the admiral, who was regarding him bleakly. Then his eyes sought out Naomi, whose gaze was stony. He looked at Marissa almost with relief. She was somehow managing to be bright and gay and charming and to ignore his own irresolution. "Yes, of course I want to see the ship—" He let it drop there. What else could he say or do before an audience?

Then Marissa insisted on a game of cards, which lasted until Naomi pleaded a headache and withdrew to her room before Erle had a chance to speak to her. Marissa mixed the three of them a drink.

"How wonderful that you can meet an old friend in a faraway place like this!" she said. "Have you known Miss

Castiliano long?"

"Yes. Well, since I met her on the *Infinity* coming to Regulus City, but in a way, you see, Miss Castiliano and I have really known each other much longer. We were associated professionally."

"You mean she's a freak?" Marissa exclaimed triumphantly, "I never would have guessed it."

"There's nothing wrong with Naomi," Erle said quickly, "She's quite normal. That is, she is *entirely* normal—like me."

The admiral was blowing smoke rings from his cigar. "I'm afraid that's more than you can say for us, dear."

Erle finished his drink and went to bed. He didn't sleep well that night, knowing what Naomi must think. Nor did he quite know how to squelch Marissa. After all, she was the admiral's wife.

The next day, out in space, dropping through the sparsely starred regions of the southern skies, Erle and Naomi were finally alone. The admiral was talking to Ekno and examining the stellar navigational atlas. Marissa was asleep.

Erle turned to Naomi. "How did you get here?" he asked, his eyes taking in every movement she made.

She smiled and stretched like a lazy lioness, her tawny legs long and beautiful. "On those little walks, directed by the glass shoes."

"It's been two weeks since we reached Metagalactic City," Erle said, "Tell me what you've been doing."

"Nothing startling. They picked me to come because I was normal...and because I had absolute pitch, which they thought might be cultivated into absolute motion, but it wasn't successful."

Erle drew on a cigarette, "And now?"

"As I understand it," she said, "among many races in the universe it is the rule that the female is as strong as the male. I think perhaps the general, knowing the bisexuality of humans, had a quaint idea that you would be better able to do your work with a woman around." She blew a cloud of smoke to the ceiling. "I'm sure it never occurred to him that humans might be *tri*sexual."

Erle's features darkened, "Naomi, quit acting like a brat."

She unleashed the fire of her sea-green eyes on him, "You said a lot of sweet things, and I fell for them. But I know now you were only warming up."

"That's not the truth. The Blomberg situation isn't what you think it is."

"I wonder if Admiral Blomberg would agree with you."

"I don't understand you, Naomi. You'd think—"

"I *do* hope you've managed to entertain each other," said Marissa, coming suddenly into the room. She sank into her chair. "Oh dear...I forgot my cigarettes. Erle, will you get them, please?"

In a few minutes he came back and tossed them in front of her. He was watching Naomi, startled by the hatred in her sea-green eyes.

"I've got to see Yjul about the test," he said, and went toward the admiral.

Fyllath was standing at one side, watching the instruments.

"I was telling the admiral," said Yjul in his buzzing voice, "that about this time tomorrow—your tomorrow that is— we'll be five hundred or so light-years from Regulus in a part of the metagalaxy where there's no scheduled traffic. The star density down here is low, giving us room to maneuver. We should pass slightly south of the Sink, a blackout space— probably a cloud of ionized magnesium gas."

"We're away from the carrier now?" asked Blomberg.

"Yes," Yjul said. "She will stand off a couple of light minutes while we maneuver."

"And no weapons," Blomberg frowned.

"What if we get lost from the mother ship?" asked Naomi.

"Not much chance of that," Yjul said softly. "However, we have a standby atomic engine and a limited quantity of fuel."

Marissa complained, "I wish we had some music."

"I suggest you all go to bed," said Yjul, "By the time you awaken we shall be in position to try for alignment."

THEY HAD FINISHED eating the next morning when Yjul sat Erle in a chair before a bank of dials. "I'll strap these instruments to your wrists. Essentially this is the same machine they used to test you, but this one is far more sensitive." He stopped and seemed to shake himself.

Erle asked, "Something wrong?"

"A little headache," said Yjul.

"I'm afraid this one isn't that simple. I got it years ago, working on this sail apparatus. I don't suppose it will leave me until it gets settled one way or another."

He finished plugging in the jacks, "Now you are free to concentrate at your leisure. When you get yourself in tune with absolute motion, the encephalo pickup and amplifier will align the sail automatically."

"Is it absolute motion or absolute rest?" asked Marissa, leaning over Erle's shoulder.

"They are the same," Yjul answered softly. "Absolute rest is a hypothetical place in stasis. It could be absolute for the Fourth Universe—the seat of the twenty-fifth dimension, if you wish to refer to your own dimensional mechanics—and not so for the Cosmos. So it's rather a paradox. It goes back to relativity, Madam Blomberg."

Marissa looked brightly uninterested. "I think," she announced, "that we all need a drink."

Yjul said, "Do you wish a drink, Mr. Bertron?"

Erle turned to see Naomi settling down at the table where she could watch the screen, "No," Erle said, "I don't."

"We are eighty-five light-seconds from the carrier," said Ekno, "and they are now paralleling us."

"Fine," said Yjul. "Whenever you are ready, Mr. Bertron."

The lights abruptly went out, and there remained only a couple of dozen pilot lights on the instrument panel. Everything was very still for a moment. Ekno stood unmoving in his pilot's horseshoe. Erle was just beginning to let go when he heard Marissa say something to Naomi in a voice too low for him to distinguish the words, but loud enough for him to wonder what she was saying.

Then he became annoyed because he was allowing her to upset him. He sat back and tried to put Marissa and Naomi out of his mind—to recover that queer rushing around him, as of black, weightless water, to find himself caught up in it and carried along so that there would be no sense of external motion. When that happened, he would be "in tune," and the primal power of the universe would flow through the engine of the *Drifter*. He remained there quietly, concentrating, forgetting, concentrating. Even the instrument panel lights winked out.

He sat there for at least a chrono, and then another. Finally he asked, "Will it have to be it stronger impulse than I experienced in the test room?"

"By no means," Yjul said softly. "With one tenth of the mental force you showed in the tests, you will be able to align us. With a good strong impulse it won't take more than a few millichrons—about one fifteenth as long as you held alignment in your tests."

Erle sat back again. He closed his eyes and tried to concentrate. But he finally realized that it was no use, and gave up the attempt.

"You might as well turn on the lights," he said. "I can't get it at all."

The lights came on. "You'll probably have better luck this

afternoon," Yjul said.

"I don't want to be temperamental about this, but somehow—" He tightened his lips. "I could always detect it until I got tired."

"The surroundings are strange," Fyllath suggested. "Perhaps if you had a little more time—"

Erle stared at her and wondered if she was reading his mind—or was it only feminine intuition?

"Never mind," said Yjul. "I will notify the mother ship." He shuffled over to Ekno, and Erle heard Ekno's low, buzzing voice, "I was in communication with the mother ship when we started the test. But apparently the contact has been broken."

Yjul stood like a statue for an instant. He asked, "Are we still at the same distance?"

"Plus or minus a few light-seconds—yes."

"Our beam will carry at least twenty light-minutes—and the mother ship's transmitter can reach us from anywhere in the Fourth Universe, unless—" He let the sentence trail off.

One of Ekno's tentacles was pressing a small button, "No response," he announced.

"How about vision?" asked Erle, "Is the *Nucleonic* still in sight?"

Ekno pointed to the screen. The background was dense black, but the *Nucleonic*, outlined by rows of glowing lights along her sleek sides, filled up most of the space...

"Sixteen million miles away," Erle noted. "It's odd they don't answer. There must be a breakdown."

Yjul shook his upper fronds, "Not on the *Nucleonic*. She has duplicate communication facilities, anyway."

The feeling of catastrophe grew on Erle and it spread through the control room. Naomi and Marissa and the admiral all came to watch. Marissa said brightly, "Don't tell me you have failed to tune in on the Mysterium Magnum."

Naomi said, "It makes my scalp prickle. There's something strange going on. I wonder if—"

She didn't finish. The screen suddenly filled with a blinding white light. Erle swung away from it. Naomi covered her eyes with her hands.

Ekno said quietly, "The *Nucleonic* has exploded. That's why I couldn't raise her. The light-waves of the explosion had not reached here yet, but the *Nucleonic* had already ceased to exist."

Blomberg, narrow-eyed, said, "That leaves us down here on our own."

"For the present—yes," Ekno said.

The screen now was filled with roily yellow and red flames and great clouds of soot. Naomi was standing close to Erle. No one said a word while the red and yellow flames folded in upon one another and suddenly winked out, leaving the screen dark.

CHAPTER TEN

"IT WAS a nuclear explosion," Yjul said soberly, "The entire ship and crew were gasefied instantly."

"Do you think something happened to her store of stygium?" Blomberg asked.

"Not from the inside," said Yjul. "Her atom stores were quadruply guarded. There is only one explanation—an attack from another ship."

"What other ship?" asked Blomberg.

"There need be no speculation over that," said Yjul. "Only one life-form in the Fourth Universe has both the desire and the resources to build such weapons, and the courage to use them to make a direct attack on a metagalactic ship."

"You mean the Alphirkians. They followed us under blackout."

"Stand by, *Drifter*!" said a sibilant voice.

They looked at the screen. Now there was a luminous background, but in place of the *Nucleonic* was the triangular head that had reared up in the snake show at Greater Galactic. The velvet black scales on the top of the great reptile's head and down the sides of its neck showed glossy in the screen. The under side of its throat was yellow. The eyes were black and the slits vertical.

"Stand by," Volmik repeated, "We are going to board you."

One of Ekno's tentacles shot at a button. "I've cut off all broadcast from the *Drifter*," he said, "We're blacked out, coasting through space at five hundred Gs. I doubt that they can board us in flight, but they probably can follow us."

"How much fuel do we have?" asked Yjul.

"About twenty-five thousand light-seconds."

"I'd like to see if they can follow us," said Yjul. "Turn on the atomic engine and set course for Alpha Hydrae. There is a radioactive planet in that group. The ore is poor, but it would enable us to get back home."

"Do you mean," asked Naomi faintly, "that we have not enough fuel of our own to get back to the populated area of the Second Metagalaxy."

"I'm sorry. We don't."

"Hell of a thing," Blomberg grumbled. "Should have sent an escort with us."

"An escort would have advised the Alphirkians what we were doing, and it would have been only a matter of time until they would get hold of a ship with the absolute motion engine in it."

"They've gotten us anyway."

"Haven't you had military training, admiral?" Yjul asked.

Blomberg took out a fresh cigar, "Sure, I know. Calculated risks. Somehow it doesn't seem as easy, now that we're looking an atomic attack in the face."

"You must be objective, general—not subjective."

Ekno was stabbing at buttons, pressing levers, turning wheels with all his fronds. Gongs clattered, buzzers sounded, and lights flashed. Erle felt the *Drifter* lurch forward.

"Try a run through the Sink," Yjul suggested. "It might throw them off. We'll never outrun them straight on," he explained. "He undoubtedly has the best ship of the Forty-third Galaxy. But we have one thing in our favor."

"I'd like to hear about that," said Blomberg.

"He wants our ship whole and he wants Mr. Bertron alive."

"What does that mean in terms of survival?"

Yjul revolved a little toward the admiral. "As a man with military training," Yjul said softly, "you will realize that the only important objective is keeping the absolute motion engine and all its factors out of the hands of Volmik."

Erle watched the admiral struggle with himself, and Erle guessed that the admiral had a few odd genes in his makeup, but the admiral came out of it. "All right. Then we run."

"We run. We can't go far on the fuel we have. We can use about a third of twenty-five thousand light-seconds for acceleration. The other will have to be saved for deceleration."

"We could drift forever at our present speed, couldn't we?" Erle asked.

"We could. But it wouldn't do us much good. We'd probably get lost in the Void somewhere below Achernar."

The sibilant voice came again. "Stand by, *Drifter*. We are coming on board."

Ekno was pushing a lever to the left, and a black needle on a dial marked "c" was moving steadily to the right; it was approaching "700."

"Tracer rays on us," Ekno said presently.

Volmik's unpleasant voice filled the pilot room, and Erle looked back of him. Even Marissa was watching, her face unusually white, "There are no other ships in this area," Volmik said, "and your communications beam will not reach the listening post on Tarazed. You started with less than twenty-five thousand light-seconds of fuel."

Yjul's leaves seemed to bristle. "Spies everywhere," he said.

"There'll certainly be a cleanup if we get back," said the admiral.

Volmik spoke again, "This is the *Axplenator*, registered from Alphirk, Forty-third Galaxy. We accuse you of piracy against the carrier ship *Nucleonic* and order you to stand by for boarding."

Yjul's answer sounded like a snort.

"Volmik is putting that on the record for his own protection," said Fyllath.

"We ought to be putting something of our own on record," said the admiral.

Yjul motioned to a tiny flickering light. "Every sound has gone into an indestructible black box."

The admiral frowned, "*How* indestructible?"

Yjul's voice was softly grating, and Erle wondered if he was finding the admiral a little trying, "There are no degrees of indestructibility," Yjul said.

"But if the *Drifter* is exploded with a nucleonic warhead, like the carrier—"

"The box and its contents are concussion-proof and non-fusible. It would merely be thrown clear, with the impetus from the explosion added to its present speed. It would travel for millions of years, but eventually it would be caught up by the gravitational power of the Fourth Universe and turned inside the curvature of space. You see, it will be found *sometime*."

"Provided," Ekno said, "that we don't get too far out of the universe before that happens."

Yjul seemed to shrug. "Then it would be found in some other universe."

"What good is it, if it can't be opened?" asked Erle.

"That's not what I said. It's indestructible, but it can be opened by bombardment with a combination of certain frequencies—the key to which is held at Intelligence on Tarazed."

"Then it seems to me it would be a dangerous thing for the Alphirkians to have in their possession."

"It would. There is no explanation for having such a box. But it isn't likely that our companions out there could find it, if that is worrying you. It's a small box, and space is rather large, out here. Also it will be traveling very fast."

"Wouldn't it be radioactive from the explosion?" the admiral asked sharply.

Yjul shook his leaves. "The material is completely inert. It will not pick up radiation. We use the same material for shielding our fuel. We couldn't use stygium at all without this. It's important to keep that in mind."

Erle looked at Naomi and wished he could say something to lessen her fears. Marissa was at a table at the other end of the cabin.

"We follow you," said Volmik. "There is no possibility of escape. In the name of the metagalaxy I order you to stand by."

"Why don't you answer them so it can go on their record?" asked the admiral.

"A waste of words. They are controlling the record as it is made—or possibly it is already made."

"Those boxes are sealed by the Space Patrol, aren't they?"

"Of course. But undoubtedly they have extras. The Alphirkians are well organized for this type of work."

Ekno was still pushing the lever, and the needle had passed 800, but now he seemed to center his attention on a different dial—probably, Erle thought, the fuel reserve.

Naomi was watching the reptilian face, still in the screen. "Are they really snakes?" she asked suddenly.

Yjul turned from the screen, "Why do you ask that?"

"Its body doesn't seem real."

Yjul watched the screen.

"You are approaching the Void," Volmik said. "You are risking the loss of your ship and crew."

Yjul said slowly, "No, Miss Castiliano, they are not snakes. We do not know what they are. They appear in many disguises—often humanoid—but they are not snakes."

"Doesn't Intelligence know what they are?" asked the admiral.

"I don't think so. Perhaps only their servants, the androids they created, know that secret. Whatever they are, they have zealously guarded their form from the rest of the universe. Their motivation has been a subject of some speculation."

"I know," Naomi announced. "They're ashamed of their own bodies."

Yjul uttered something that sounded like a chuckle. "Your intuition is extremely sharp, Miss Castiliano."

Ekno said without turning, "We can't make Alpha Hydrae. Our fuel supply has been tampered with."

Yjul whirled. "You said twenty-five thousand—"

"The gauges showed that much. But they were wrong too. Now look at them."

The needle was getting close to a red area.

"You can't depend on it, though. We don't know how much we do have."

"I have just made a radiation check. There are about four thousand available light-seconds left."

Yjul said slowly, "Why not head into the Sink? It's twenty light-years long, and it might be the *Axplenator* will not be able to keep a tracer on us in there?"

Ekno dropped the acceleration lever and touched one of a row of keys. Above the quartz window Erle saw the left half of a circle of blue lights go dead, and at the same time he felt a pull to that side. Ekno was turning the *Drifter* with half a ring. A moment later Volmik's face on the screen became blurred and wavy, and Yjul nodded. "At least there's interference from that ionized magnesium, though there's probably not one atom per cubic mile."

"Why don't we turn back inside the cloud?" asked the admiral.

"In twenty light-years, at our speed." Yjul shook his head. "We haven't the fuel."

The admiral's face reddened. He spun on his heel and went out.

Naomi turned to Yjul. "If we do lose them in the Sink, what do we do then?" she asked. "We haven't enough fuel to go back, and we haven't enough food to spend millions of years traveling the curvature of the universe."

"This may not be news to you, Miss Castiliano," Yjul said gravely, "but I have been wondering that myself."

Erle looked at Naomi. "And if we did have the food, where would we put the grandchildren?"

She stared belligerently at him. "What grandchildren?"

After what seemed like a minute or two, Yjul said, "We're out of the cloud, and coasting? Would you like to try the alignment again?"

"Yes," Erle said. He wished Naomi would stay near him, but she turned her back and went to join Marissa and the admiral.

He got into the chair and was strapped up with the machine. The lights went out. "No collision objects ahead, according to the atlas," Ekno reported.

"What's our course?" asked Yjul.

"Position minus thirty-three degrees declination, at four hours and fifty-five minutes right ascension, radial velocity positive at twenty-two light-seconds per second, trajectory minus forty-eight degrees, relativistic velocity one thousand, one hundred G's."

Erle began to concentrate. For a little while he thought he was going to get it, but at the very last minute the picture of Naomi walking away from him popped into his mind and threw him off. Presently he tried again, but this time it was a memory of Marissa. Then he thought of Naomi again—her platinum hair and green eyes, her lovely legs, the way she had kissed him on the *Infinity*.

He awoke with Yjul unfastening the wrist contacts. "I'm sorry," Erle said, "I must have gone to sleep."

"Perhaps you can try later."

Erle went to the table. The admiral looked at him, "No luck, eh?"

Erle shook his head.

The admiral poured a drink, "No doubt our bones will be floating around down at the bottom of the universe for the next couple of millennia."

"There's hope," said Erle, "It looks as if we've thrown off the *Axplenator* anyway."

But a crackling came from the screen. Volmik's ugly head filled the glass, "How do you expect to get away?" he asked. "We can track you by your radiation."

They sank into silence then. Yjul, Fyllath, and Ekno remained at the controls, mostly standing quietly and staring into space.

The admiral lit a cigar; his hands were unsteady. He

looked at Marissa with her head on her arms on the table, and rose with a great weariness resting upon him. It was visible in his tormented eyes, the slump of his shoulders.

"Must get her to bed," he said. Then he looked at Erle. "You carry her. I'll never make it."

Erle glanced at Naomi and saw the scorn in her eyes. But he rose slowly. If he got rid of these two, he told himself, he could be alone with Naomi and talk. He picked up Marissa and carried her quickly to her bedroom and laid her on the bed. The admiral had followed. Erle shut the door on them and returned to Naomi.

She was smoking a cigarette. She got up and tossed her cigarette into the disintichute.

"And we may not get away either," she said; referring to Volmik's threat, "unless you get your mind off *her* and remember what you came out here for—Mr. Man With Absolute Motion!"

Erle stared at her face. A double row of small spots shone like silver on her cheeks. They were tears, but what good did that do him? She walked out with her head high.

He poured himself a drink. With 400 billion inhabited planets in the metagalaxy, with 500 billion metagalaxies in the universe, and with 208 billion universes in the Cosmos, the probability of any two given persons coming together in the same ship was so remote as to be utterly inconceivable—and yet he was here, and so was Marissa.

CHAPTER ELEVEN

ERLE SLEPT FINALLY with his head on the table, but awoke to hear that sibilant voice from the screen. He got up, feeling beaten all over, and went forward.

"I am warning you. Stand by or we shall destroy you."

"We could surrender," said Yjul, "and probably be well

treated."

"Surrender?" Erle stared at Yjul. "Never heard the word."

Ekno chuckled. He pushed the lever and the *Drifter* lurched forward, "We'll drive down into the Deeps," Yjul said. "They don't dare to follow us forever."

"The Stellar Survey hasn't charted the Deeps, has it?"

"No."

"Is there a possibility of finding fuel?"

"Speculative."

"If we don't, it'll be a long way home."

"Unless," Fyllath murmured, "we can get the engine aligned. If we get that in velocital synchronization, we can outrun anything in the Fourth Universe."

"If we don't," Yjul pointed out, "none of us will live long enough to talk about it—for even *we* don't live forever."

They reached a velocity of 1900 G's before Ekno's gray-green tentacle released the lever, "We haven't lost the *Axplenator*," he said, "but we're out in front."

"He isn't on the screen," said Erle.

"No, but I'm getting plenty of blips on the ultrawave. He's back there all right. He must have a powerful tracer."

"How's the fuel?"

"I've used just about all I dare. Providing we do get away, we'll have to allow for some directional bursts, and we'll have to cut down this terrific velocity."

"We can't outrun them, I'm afraid," said Yjul.

Ekno shook his head and said, "They're gaining on us now. They've got a good ship and plenty of fuel."

"If we used our fuel to reverse course, we'd have none left to accelerate," Fyllath noted, "Then it would be only a matter of time until they'd tie onto us. And we cannot afford to spend more fuel on acceleration, for at such terrific velocity as we are now traveling the only way to stop without ample fuel is to be taken in by a carrier ship."

Erle lit a cigarette, "You cheer me," he said.

"I've always wondered," Fyllath said softly, "what was on the other side of the Deeps. Is it really the Second Universe, where our race is supposed to have originated back in the mists of pre-cosmic time, or might it be the Third Universe, where all natural laws are the opposite of those in the Fourth? Has the Second reached a state of entropy so that it's all run down—or is there just nothing at all down there?"

"As an academic question," said Yjul. "I like it—but I'm not eager to find the answer empirically."

"We have no choice," said Erle, "unless I can get back on the beam." He stepped forward and got in the chair.

Yjul and Fyllath fastened the wrist contacts, and Yjul worked the controls as the lights went out. Erle tried to concentrate. He tried very hard, but always, at the last moment, he would think of Naomi or Marissa, or both, and all power of sensing the primal motion would leave him.

Fyllath said softly, "It is the kind of thing where one must be calm and relaxed and sure of himself."

Erle looked at her. Then he got up and went to his bed.

When he awoke, Naomi was eating breakfast alone. "Mind if I sit down with you?" he asked.

"It's as much your ship as mine," she retorted, "Anyway, I'm almost through." She looked toward the admiral's room. Somebody had closed the door, and there were sounds of activity.

"Listen," he said. "This has gone far enough," He stood before her, "What if we have to stay down here the rest of our lives?"

"Then you're going to have trouble with Marissa," Naomi said sweetly, "for she will be very restless!"

A few minutes later by apparent time, or a week later by relativistic time, a number of years by Earth time, or minus

132 chronos by life-time, they were a thousand megaparsecs from Regulus City, in the unknown Deeps at the bottom of the Fourth Universe—a fantastic halfworld of black cosmic wastes where material bodies didn't average one in a million cubic parsecs. Erle was still trying to align the motion engine, and still tailing, and they were still coasting.

"There's a blue star ahead," laid Naomi. "Is that Achernar? Could it possibly be—"

Yjul was thumbing the *Astrotator*. "There's not much positive information on Achernar. Magnitude minus point six, although it doesn't say whether that is absolute. Spectral type eighty-five and that means a very hot star. Various unsubstantiated reports give Achernar a planetary system of over a hundred major bodies. High-level radioactivity has been supposedly detected. No Stellar Survey report available."

Yjul slapped the big book shut. "It isn't much."

Ekno said, "If we stay on course we'll be caught in Achernar's gravitational pull."

"We may as well," said Yjul. "We've got to get help some way or we'll never get home. There's no star system below Achernar."

"Is anybody even sure," asked Fyllath, "that Achernar is in the Fourth Universe?"

Yjul shivered, but he rested some of his fronds on the instrument board and slowly shook his top.

Erle said, "We'd better try again."

He tried but it didn't work. Naomi stayed on the opposite side of the control room, while Marissa and the admiral finished their breakfast.

Ekno threw the *Drifter* into a cometary orbit and reduced speed for a maximum of observation. Achernar was some twenty-four times the diameter of the Sun, and the ten nearest planets were gaseous or molten. But out about the twenty-fifth planet, the worlds began to cool off, and there was some suggestion of green.

"Probable landing spots," said Ekno.

"No indication of radiating elements," said Yjul. "We'd better keep moving."

The ship had entered Achernar's system at an orbital inclination of 32 degrees, and kept swinging around the star and back through the planets, while Yjul and Fyllath checked spectrographs for oxygen, water, or carbon dioxide, and watched the counters for radioactivity.

On the eighth trip around, Yjul finished his gingerbread notes in the logbook and said, "There's still one left— Achernar XCIV."

"We'll hit it the next trip," said Ekno.

They swung around in a tremendous elliptical curve. The Vaulet counter rippled with static and burst into a rattle. Then the planet was behind, and Ekno and Yjul were staring at each other.

"That's it!" said Ekno. "Terrific radiation. Heavy elements—maybe even stygium."

"Can we land?" asked Fyllath. "Is there solid matter?"

"Fairly high temperature," said Yjul, "but we can stand it. The Gruttman shields will protect us from radiation."

"We might be able to live there." Marissa said, gay again, "but what would we do for entertainment?"

"Solid matter," thought Erle, "Solid matter" could be molten stone, for instance. That was "solid," wasn't it? And what about the atmosphere? Would there be breathable air, or would it be, say, hydrogen cyanide, one breath of which would kill them, or perhaps pure fluorine, savagely corrosive?

Erle kept still, but he realized, and he knew the Gamma Velorum people understood, that the only chance was to find a radioactive mineral, get it on board quickly, and move on. It was entirely possible that the only breathable oxygen, would be the supply which they carried themselves.

The nose gauge began to show considerable temperature. "I'm letting it heat," Ekno explained, "to save fuel. There's a heavy atmosphere, and it will help to slow us down."

The sonar gauge showed 18,000 meters above the surface of the planet. They swung twice around, steadily decelerating.

Below the clouds, Erle pointed to a great spout of black ash and red-hot rock. "Lots of volcanic activity," he said.

"To be expected from a planet with radioactive content. There'll be constant earthquakes and terrific storms. We may not even be able to get out of the ship."

"I'm getting chlorophyll lines," said Fyllath.

"Then there's oxygen. That sounds friendly."

"I'd like to park next to some nice, quiet volcano that isn't mad at anybody," Naomi said hopefully.

They put on space suits that looked like long underwear made of gray silk, with mechanical three-fingered hands. "The aerial on top is to receive power broadcast from the ship to operate all the various functions of your suits," explained Yjul. "Watch out when the red light glows. That mean's you're getting too far away, or the power supply from the ship is getting low."

"What furnishes power from the ship?" Erle asked abruptly.

"The fuel that is left."

Erle didn't have to ask more. He knew just how little fuel remained.

"There's a small emergency powerpak that will carry you for a while."

Naomi shuddered. She laughed a little hysterically. "What if the powerpak goes? Do we walk into the first cigar store and ask for a refill?"

Yjul looked at her, alarmed by her pallor. "There are many things that can be done," he said, reassuringly, "One must never give up."

Erle nodded.

A moment later the *Drifter*, with one last burst of power from the under rings, settled into a grove of giant ferns.

The seismograph showed continuous volcanic activity, but Yjul unsealed the outer door of the airlock. "The gravity will be heavy, I think, but the Healey units will make it possible for us to move."

Naomi made a grimace.

"I must warn you that we are under water—but don't be frightened."

"I'm not frightened," said Naomi. "I'm scared to death." But she refused to look at Erle.

The water flowed into the airlock and rose around them. It was warm and brown looking. Yjul went out first. Presently they heard his voice in their earphones, "There's a little drop about the height of a man. Set your Healeys at six point one."

They stepped off into the water. Where they were, twenty feet below the surface, there was a ghostly half-light from the great ferns. There was also an occasional thump that shook the muddy ground, and rumbles that made the surface of the water shimmer as they played their lights up at it.

A great gout of red fire leaped out of the earth far ahead of them and lit up this strange world. For a moment the crater looked like the nozzle of a giant blowtorch. Cubic miles of ash were belched up to blot out the fire. Tremendous clouds of sooty black smoke poured up as the fire died away. They were in sudden darkness, only a little relieved presently by the faint luminance of a sun twelve billion miles distant.

They moved carefully, feeling their way among the trunks of the giant ferns, sometimes walking on solidified lava, sometimes knee-deep in slime. A tremendous clap of thunder struck the water with a crash. For a moment Erle was dizzy. He looked for Naomi, but she was standing calmly, watching the surface above.

"According to the time lapse, the volcano is twenty-nine kilometers away," said Yjul. "We'll divide into two parties and work toward the volcano. Say about twenty chronos going out and twenty coming back. Watch your counters for indications of radioactive ore."

Their helmets broke water and they came out on solid rock.

"It was comfortable down there," said Naomi. "I expected it to be hot."

Yjul looked at her curiously. "Do you know the temperature of that water?"

"No, I—"

"One hundred and two degrees Centigrade."

"That's over boiling," said Erle.

"Not on this planet."

"You mean," asked Naomi, "that we walked through boiling water over our heads?"

"Your suits refrigerate," Yjul told her, "Now you and Mr. Bertron slant off to the left. We'll go to the right. Watch your Mueller counters. They are set on the number thirty, and anything that comes through will be hard radiation."

They didn't find it that day or the next, or the third. They sat around that night; Marissa and the admiral had not left the ship and were somewhat drunk. There were only three bottles of Scotch left.

"How much more power do we have left?" Naomi asked.

"Not too much," Yjul admitted. "If we don't find something tomorrow it will look pretty hopeless, for it would take power and time to mine the stuff and load it in the ship after we find it."

They christened the planet that night. With three fourths of their allotted time gone, and only one day left for exploration, they held a small celebration.

"I propose a toast," said Erle, "to the new planet."

"It should have a name," Fyllath agreed.

"Why not call it Orphan?" asked Naomi. "It's surely a long way from its parent."

CHAPTER TWELVE

ERLE OMITTED shaving the next morning to save power, "An erg is an erg," he told Yjul. He was feeling pretty good, for Naomi seemed more friendly.

"You are right," Yjul said. "The energy required to run that apparatus might make the difference between life or death."

It was on that day they discovered that The Orphan had three moons, for they all came up together. Each was different size and they moved at different speeds, being hardly more than light gray disks against a darker sky. A few hours after they saw the moons they decided there were no mobile forms of life anywhere on the planet. There were algae, but no fish, no eels, no amphibians.

"Apparently The Orphan is not ready for animal life yet," said Yjul.

That night they were glum. "We've found nothing that could be called a deposit," Yjul reminded them.

"Tomorrow," said Ekno, "we'd better keep the ship closed up. We can live for fifty or sixty days if we conserve energy."

"That won't do us any good," Erle contended, "What chance is there of another ship's crossing the Deeps in the next sixty days? And if it did, what makes you think it could find us on a world of this size? And we must eat—we're no century plants."

Yjul shook his head sadly. "We could not live much longer than you. When our power supply is gone, the ship will no longer be refrigerated. How long do you think we can endure temperatures above that of boiling water?"

"Not only that," said Fyllath. "The Orphan is having a period of comparative quiet right now. The temperature could easily go up a hundred degrees outside if volcanic activity increases in this area."

Erle looked at them, "Sorry," he said.

Already it seemed unusually warm inside the ship. The humidity gauge said 50, and Erle had to keep wiping the dampness from his forehead. The last bottle of Scotch stood nine-tenths empty on the table between Marissa and the admiral.

Erle said, "Once there was a tri-di called *Orphans of the Storm*. They could do one on us called *Orphans of The Orphan*. It would be ironic, at the very least."

Nobody laughed. Naomi looked pale and strained. She was starting to say something when Marissa got up. She reached Erle with the bottle of Scotch in one hand, "There's enough in here for one more drink," she said, "I propose a toast to the Man with Absolute Motion—and he should drink it." She thrust the bottle at him.

Erle pushed it away.

Naomi was staring at the thermometer in the center of the control room, "Rather than sit here and wait," Erle said, "I say let's keep looking for ore. You've forgotten one thing, Yjul."

The tall Gamma Velorumite seemed to be pressing what must have been his head with one leaf. He looked around, "What's that?"

"There's still enough power for four days exploration. We might as well use it, because if we find ore, one of us can bring back enough in our hands to keep the power plant going while we dig more."

Ekno nodded, "And there's still the possibility that you might be able to align the sail to make it functional again."

Erle looked at Marissa, and then at Naomi, who had her back turned. It was a fantastic situation. With so much dependent on the alignment of the sailpack, these two women were exerting too much effect on his efforts.

THEY DID not find fuel the next day or the next. On the third day, as they were resting at the far end of their route, Yjul said, "The volcanic activity is increasing. We might expect almost anything—submersion in red-hot lava, a fissure opening up under us—almost anything. So it is as well we have used our power this way."

Erle said, "Have we covered all the possible ground?"

"All but one segment. I was saving that for tomorrow."

Somehow Erle found Naomi's hand in his, and he took a deep breath. They rested for a little longer, saying nothing, watching the crater belch fire and smoke ahead of them. Stealing glances at Naomi's face as it reflected the red light of the volcano, Erle thought that—strangely enough—he had never been quite as happy as he was at that moment. He had suffered a great deal from her aloofness, and now, he hoped, there would be no more of that.

They reached the ship and all went in together. "One more day's power left," Yjul said as they got out of their suits. "Maybe you'd better try the sail again, Mr. Bertron—before it's too late. It will take power to amplify your thought-force, you know."

Erle looked at Naomi. She smiled at him, and he felt wonderful. Yes, he could do it now; he knew he could, "Strap me in," he said.

Yjul fastened the connections on his wrists. The lights

went low and Erle began to concentrate. *This time*, he thought, *this time was it*. Naomi was standing at his side. Yes, this time he would put it over.

Suddenly Marissa, too, was at his side, her hand on his shoulder, "Do you really think you can do it?" she asked, and her voice, smooth as it may have been, grated on him.

"Why don't you let me alone?" he asked harshly.

Marissa looked up at him, then went away slowly. Naomi walked to the airlock and stared at the volcano.

Erle sat there for a few minutes. Then he took the wrist connectors off and slammed them down, "I can't do it tonight. It would be a waste of power to try."

He got up and went to bed.

In the morning they adjusted their suits and left in silence. Yjul had checked the fuel. They had one more day—no more.

They had almost reached the end of their journey when a call came from Yjul and Fyllath. "We've got something here! It looks good! If you can cut across a couple of kilometers, we'll take back all we can carry."

They had two radiation hammers and four collapsible Healey units, and it didn't take long to fill them. The red lights began to glow as they waded into the swamp, but they made it through the airlock. Ekno helped them load the jagged pieces of ore in the bin. When they had finished, Yjul was sitting down. It was the first time Erle had ever seen him assume such a position.

"Headache?" Erle asked.

"Splitting," said Yjul.

"Well, hang together. We'll be off of this planet soon."

"Now that the immediate problem appears near a solution, I can't help thinking about the only really important problem. Our small, individual lives are nothing compared to the future of the metagalaxy."

The next day they brought in two large loads of ore with the aid of the Healeys. Ekno went with them and surveyed the deposit. "There's plenty here. All we have to do is get it in the ship."

His leaves fluttered as the ground thundered under them, and he looked up at the volcano. "Before that thing blows up the planet," he added.

In three more days they had a sizable supply in the bins. Three days after that they had enough to take the *Drifter* back to the populated portions of the universe.

They loaded their carryalls for the last time, never taking their eyes off the volcano. Rolling clouds of fire and smoke were being blown into the sky with steady, tremendous violence. The swamp was beginning to bubble and steam.

Erle fell back to help Naomi lift a foot from the sucking mud. He heard Ekno say sharply in Regulian: *"Angon ambeta sto?"*

Erle straightened. That was the metagalactic challenge.

"There was something moving in the water ahead of us," Ekno said, "The mud is still swirling."

They cut off their lights and made their way cautiously through the water, winding in and out among the softly glistening trunks of the ferns. Then the red light began to glow in the top of Erle's fishbowl. Around him, the other three showed red lights too.

"Somebody has taken control of the ship!" shouted Yjul. "They are cutting off the power."

"Surely not Marissa and the admiral."

Erle shook his head, "They don't know enough. Switch on your emergency packs."

"We must assume," said Ekno, "that somehow the Alphirkians have reached our ship and have gotten control of it, but there is one factor in our favor. They want Mr. Bertron too."

"Then we can make at trade," Erle said, "I go on board only if they let the rest of you on the ship."

The ground was rumbling under them until it was hard to stand. Back through the water, Erle could see that a great fissure had opened in the side of the crater, and molten rock was boiling out of it.

Ekno made a reconnaissance of the ship. "There is a third person in the engine room," he said, "My guess is they are trying to figure out how to convert the broadcast power plant over to impulsion."

"Let's go in," said Yjul.

Ekno looked back at the crater and watched a cubic mile of rock and ash hurtle into the air, "I'm afraid we aren't accomplishing anything out here. Volmik—if that *is* Volmik—has cut off the broadcast, and it is only a matter of time until he gets the power switched over to the atomic unit."

"With an uninhibited volcano behind us," Naomi said, "it doesn't seem that we have any choice."

They helped Yjul up, and he opened the outer door of the airlock and looked through the inner glass. One of his leaves stabbed a button in the wall, and Yjul said with a sigh, "Come on up. He's in the engine room, and I have closed the bulkhead against him. He can never get out now."

They climbed up and stood in the airlock while the compressed nitrogen blew the water out. Then Yjul opened the inner door. They went inside. A burst of fire from the crater lighted up The Orphan and threw weird red shadows over the control room. Marissa and the admiral were sitting there. Then the ship was shaken from the concussion of the last explosion and scorched by the blast of heat. The strange smell of bromine lingered in the control room.

Erle ran to the bulkhead. Inside, Volmik's huge reptilian body lay on the floor among the bins and the engine, and his six hands were busy on the controls. Ekno and Yjul had run to the control panel of the ship, and Erle turned back in time to see Fyllath falling back before a strange man with dead white face and a red fringe of hair.

It was Jastrow. Naomi started for him, but Erle got there first. He hit him on the chin twice, but Jastrow didn't even grunt. He got hold of the man's throat and began to strangle him. He felt him go limp, and then a strange thing happened. Jastrow began to dissolve. His neck went to nothingness under Erle's fingers. He became a cloud of smoke that rolled in upon itself, becoming swiftly smaller and smaller.

Jastrow's red fringe of hair looked out from the ball of smoke, and his black eyes gleamed with malevolence. Then the ball rolled across the floor and through the bulkhead. Erle ran to look through. The smoke was sucked into the nostrils of the snake and disappeared. Erle felt sick.

The ship was rocking violently. Water splashed on its sides, and the frame shuddered, "Don't you think," said Fyllath, "we'd better get under way?"

"Sorry," Ekno said. "Somehow he's preventing us from getting power. Probably he hasn't figured out the combination yet."

Naomi looked at the bulkhead and shivered. "What happened to Jastrow?"

"I think," said Yjul, "Jastrow was Volmik's other self. He could form into anything Volmik wanted, but he did not dare to be out of the Alphirkian's body when he died, or he'd have to roam space forever in that form—and I have no doubt the humanoid form is repulsive to them."

The ship was rocking as blast after blast lighted up The Orphan with red fire, while concussion after concussion shook the *Drifter*. The wind was coming up and hurling steady sheets of brown water at the ship's sides.

Erle said, "Give me a weapon—anything, a chair leg, an

empty liquor bottle. Hurry! Somebody has got to go in there and get rid of that thing."

"You couldn't do it," said Yjul. "Volmik has powers beyond any of us. You wouldn't get through the bulkhead—and then we'd all be at his mercy!"

Erle was at the bulkhead now, looking through the round plastic window. His face had gone deathly pale.

"That's one of their androids!" Yjul exclaimed, "They've been threatening to revolt for ten thousand years!"

A humanoid form was standing amidst the bins and engines. The humanoid had an air shovel in its hands, and was stabbing at the snake. Volmik kept weaving from side to side, trying to fix his terrible slitted eyes on the android's eyes, and Volmik's puny yellowish hands kept reaching for the android's sides.

"Why doesn't he coil around the android and crush him?" asked Naomi.

"I doubt that he has any real constrictive power in that artificial body," said Yjul. "The Alphirkians seem always to have controlled their androids by voice and mind."

"He isn't doing it now," Eire noted.

"No. It is not the first time an artificially created being has assumed volition," Yjul observed. "You put certain units together—it doesn't make any difference whether they are flesh and blood or electrical—and you induce certain impulses through them for countless thousands of years, to the effect that the total unit or being moves by itself and performs actions initiated only by the impulses. It is not astonishing that eventually the impulse-paths, becoming well worn, induce the impulses of their own accord.

"Eventually some of these impulses will take independent paths, and you then have a creature with initiative. I think that's what has happened here. The Alphirkians were warned of this by metagalactic officials a long time ago, but for some reason they refused to have any living being on their planet except themselves. We have never understood that. Perhaps we never shall."

The ship rocked violently. Volmik was now grasping the android's wrists with four of its hands, while the other two were pawing the android in what would have been the kidney region of a human. The android tried to get the air shovel aimed at the snake's neck, just back of its head. But the puny arms showed surprising strength, and the android seemed unable to overcome them. Also it seemed mortally afraid of the damage that might be done to it by the lowest pair of hands, and kept twisting away.

A constant flickering red fire from the volcano lighted up the interior of the control room.

"The temperature is rising," Ekno said, his voice shrill with alarm, "Molten lava is pouring into the water."

"There's nothing we can do," Yjul said, "until something happens in the engine room."

"Why not blow them out of there with a blast of compressed nitrogen?"

Yjul turned a little. "Why not?"

Erle said, "I hate to see the android kicked out when he's putting up such a battle."

Yjul asked curiously, "Would you rather risk being destroyed by the volcano?"

Erle said, "No matter what it is, when it's fighting for its life, it ought to have a chance."

Yjul said, "Some of the characteristics you exhibit are remarkably un-human."

Erle shrugged, "Not necessarily," he said. "In earlier days my characteristics were widespread. The trouble is, I'm normal."

"Normal would mean that self-preservation comes first." Fyllath looked at Erle curiously, "That's the most normal characteristic in the metagalaxy."

Erle didn't look at them. He was watching the fight in the engine room. "Let's call it a 'cultured' normal. My normality doesn't go back past the historic period."

"Call it anything," Ekno said. "The ship is settling. If it gets deep into the mud, our tubes will be fouled and we'll never get out of here."

Erle took a deep breath. "All right. Blow them out." He noted with satisfaction that Naomi was clinging to his arm. He looked at her, and could see that their minds were as one.

"I only hope," said Naomi fervently, "that he cuts the snake's head off."

At that moment the android planted the sharp edge of the air shovel behind the snake's arms and pulled the trip-trigger. The shovel went through the snake's body, leaving it attached by only a shred of skin.

"It's artificial," Fyllath pointed out. "That's flexible metal, and there are wires running down from the head."

The snake's body was curled around a stanchion, but now, as the head was severed, the body went limp. One of the lowest hands, still pawing the android, seemed to find a soft place in the android's body. It sank in, remained embedded for a moment, and then the android suddenly lost all motion and stood as if quick-frozen. The little yellow hand came out with a bundle of wires.

At that moment Erle hated the Alphirkian with an intensity he never had felt toward anyone.

The first blast of nitrogen swept through the engine room, and the android, still rigid in the attitude he had had when he was disconnected, was blown over and swept away through the hatch. The blast tore at the snake's body, now no longer tight around the stanchion, but lying limp and helpless. The snake's head stared at them through the circular glass. The vivid intensity of its slitted black eyes was fading. With one last effort the head twisted itself back. Its great mouth opened, and it buried its teeth in the stanchion.

The nitrogen tore at the metallic body. The "skin" connecting it to the head was ripped, and the body skidded across the floor and through the open hatch, propelled by the pressure of the gas into the murky brown water.

Yjul took his finger from the button, "All but the head. Shall we—"

"No!" said Ekno. "The head may contain the thing!"

"Unlikely," Fyllath pointed out. "Its eyes are glazed over."

"It could be a trick," said Erle.

"Trick or not," Yjul said firmly, "we have got to get in there and connect the engine."

He began to unbolt the door. The surface of The Orphan now was shuddering with long and violent spasms. The ship was settling deeper with every move. Erle helped, and they swung open the bulkhead.

Naomi, staring at the "dead" head of the snake, threw her hand to her mouth. She flung herself at Erle and put her head against his chest, her arms clinging to him convulsively. "Worms!" she exclaimed, "The thing is already turning into worms!"

Erle stared. One small White worm was emerging from the head. Yjul darted into the engine room and began to throw levers and breaker switches. The ship was, tossed from side to side and up out of the mud. Then it began to settle again. The white worm-like thing was crawling down the stanchion. It reached the floor and started for the open bulkhead. They stood back, fascinated.

Then Yjul called in a despairing voice, "The nitrogen blew the fuel away! We haven't enough left to get out of the water."

But for a moment they watched the worm. Something about it held them spellbound. Erle felt a hypnotic trance coming over him, but he couldn't do anything about it. They all stood back a step as the worm progressed into the center of the room. Yjul came up, and stood motionless, his fronds rigid.

The worm reached the center of the control room and turned. Its tiny head reared high, and Erle began to hear words in his mind: "You will all obey me. I am Volmik II, ruler of Alphirk and the Forty-third Galaxy. You—Yjul—gather what fuel is left and feed it into the engine. You, Ekno, go to the controls. The rest of you will go to your respective places and make no attempt to interfere. Any hesitation on your part will subject you to instant punishment by ultrasonic vibrations."

They stood as if dazed. Then Yjul went back to the engine room. Ekno moved to the controls. Fyllath went to her position. Erle and Naomi moved sidewise and started to sit down at the table with Marissa and the admiral.

The admiral's head was raised. His bleary eyes looked at the worm. "Alphirkian, eh? Volmik II, eh?" He got unsteadily to his feet. "This is one time I can do a good deed for my metagalaxy. Frankly, I welcome the opportunity."

He staggered toward the worm. Erle felt the tremendous force of the Alphirkian's mental powers lifting as it directed all of its dynamic energy at the admiral.

But the admiral's brain was too fogged by liquor to be subject to it, or perhaps the liquor had removed his inhibitions and he could be his normal self. He continued to walk straight toward the worm, which reared its head still higher.

The little, round-faced man lifted one foot above the worm, and then all the vibrant force of the worm's sonic radiation must have hit him. Erle saw the admiral die on one foot, his other in midair. His eyes went glazed and his muscles went slack, but the upraised foot descended. There was a sharp smack, and the inner juices of the worm squirted out from under the admiral's foot. The admiral fell over on the floor.

"A worm!" Naomi cried. "No wonder they didn't want anybody to know what they looked like!"

CHAPTER THIRTEEN

YJUL RUSHED FROM the engine room shaking his head. "We'll never make it. There just isn't enough fuel."

Erle looked at Naomi and touched her arm. She looked back at him, and suddenly dropped her forehead in his hand. Erle felt the power of, a great purpose within him. He jumped up and went to the chair at the instrument board. "Strap me in," he said to Yjul.

Yjul began to work. "How much time?" he asked Ekno.

"We seem to have hung up temporarily—probably

cushioned by the ferns," Ekno said. "But we can't hang here very long."

He looked toward the volcano. The entire visible area of The Orphan now was almost afire. Steam bubbled steadily up through the water around them, and even the trunks of the ferns were becoming black and shriveled under the heat.

Yjul turned down the lights. "Try to concentrate," he urged.

Erle began to slip into the familiar pattern. He closed his eyes, and the black currents started to flow around him.

Marissa's voice was in his ear: "Good old Erle. You'll get us out of here, won't you, Erle darling?"

Her arms were around his neck from behind. His hands, fastened in the connectors, could not be raised, and he could only shrug and look toward Naomi for understanding. She had jumped to her feet. For a moment she seemed about to attack Marissa. Then, her sea-green eyes blazing, her lips compressed, she turned away and went to the airlock door. She stood there and stared toward the volcano.

Erle said, "Go away, Marissa. Go away. I'll get us out of here—but go away!"

Fyllath led Marissa back to the table, and Erle tried to settle back and concentrate again, but Naomi was still staring out through the airlock, and though he tried to will her to turn around, she did not.

He turned back to his task and tried to concentrate. A new series of concussions hit the ship and tossed it one way and then the other.

"We went to forty-three degrees inclination that time," said Ekno, "I doubt that we can maintain our equilibrium much longer."

The deck was pitching and yawing, and the ship was heaving violently as if in consecutive troughs of a great sea. Erle, strapped in his chair, was fixed, but he looked for

Naomi. She was on the floor, skidding to the opposite side of the control room. Yjul was after her and helped her to her feet.

Erle tried to catch her eyes, but she refused to look at him. He wondered about Marissa, and saw that she had fallen to the floor and become wedged among the legs of the table. She now lay there limp, her head rolling from side to side as the floor went up on one side and then slid down, up on the other and again down.

Once more Erle tried to concentrate on his task, but Marissa's scornful sea-green eyes were everywhere in his mind.

A rain of molten rock and heavy debris began to fall on the ship; The lava hissed into the water and streamed down the sides of the ship.

Ekno looked at Erle. "At least we'll be decently buried," he said.

Erle knew it was no use. He had done what he could, but it wasn't enough. They'd be cooked in a solid matrix of lava, but the agony, at least, would be over in a matter of seconds.

BY THIS TIME the Bryd had become restless. What had been a very cozy, warm, pleasant mind for a quiet sleep had now turned into something of a madhouse, and the Bryd had been having nightmares. Restful minds had been hard enough to find the last few thousand years, and the Bryd had felt very proud of itself for finding Erle Bertron's mind. However, now it looked as though it would be forced to move again.

It began to probe around in Erle's mind, and before long it was quite astonished at some of the things it found there. It saw the belching volcano, the quaking ground, the steaming water, and the rain of red-hot lava, and flinched.

The Bryd looked around the control room. It detected the

three from Gamma Velorum, and after a brief excursion into their minds wondered what had gotten into them to tie up with a crackpot like this Bertron fellow.

It saw Marissa's body twisting among the legs of the table as the ship tossed about, and made a quick examination. Marissa, whoever she was, had died of an epileptic seizure—had choked to death on her tongue. She wasn't human anyway. She was a special android made by the Alphirkians and endowed with all human characteristics, even neuroticism, to serve as a spy for Volmik. Her system was saturated with alcohol, and the Bryd came out reeling.

The Bryd found the admiral's body, and it took about one tenth of a millichron to figure that one out. The admiral had died too. The Bryd looked around and found the remains of the Alphirkian on the floor.

A quiver passed over it.

The Bryd went back to Erle's mind, and then, really beginning to awaken, it discovered Erle's apparent despair. It saw that Erle's distress had something to do with a female named Naomi.

The Bryd thought things over for an instant. If Erle wanted Naomi, why wasn't he getting her? Well, obviously even to the Bryd, that failure could be directly related to some opposition from Naomi. The Bryd took a quick hop-skip to Naomi's mind and was astounded at what it found there. The woman was eating her heart out for this Erle fellow.

Somewhat puzzled, the Bryd went back to Erle's mind. Yes, the fellow wanted her. Marissa really played no part in what he wanted, even though he didn't know she was dead. The weather, it decided, was somewhat violent even for a primitive planet like The Orphan. It was getting ready to blow itself apart.

It wasn't cozy in Bertron's mind anymore, and it wasn't comfy. It might as well have picked a neurotic mind. The

Bryd sighed. Naomi was jealous of Marissa. Humans hadn't changed very much in fifty thousand years.

Well, what to do? The Bryd decided to implant the knowledge of Marissa's death in Naomi's mind, and sat back to await results. Naomi continued to lie face down on her bed, shedding tears. It went a little deeper into Naomi's mind and implanted firmly the knowledge that Erle loved her.

Suddenly Naomi turned over, got to her feet, steadied herself against the heaving floor, and rushed outside. She dashed across the floor and fell into Erle's arms, sobbing. Erle's wrists were still fastened and he couldn't put his arms around her, but that didn't seem to make any difference. She didn't say a word, nor did Erle.

The Bryd was well satisfied with the rosy warmth that flooded over Erle's mind, but it took a quick look over its shoulder and saw the ground arising outside in the beginning of a mighty blow-off. In about two seconds, it saw, there would be a chasm under the ship that would reach clear to the center of The Orphan.

The Bryd burrowed a little deeper into Erle's mind. With Naomi still hanging on him, the Bryd did a brief job on the lobe of Erle's brain that had to do with his sense of absolute motion. It made sure that Erle, filled with this blessed radiant warmth generated by his contact with Naomi, started concentrating on the black currents. The Bryd could have told them a much easier way of detecting absolute motion, but that wasn't within its policy.

Erle went to work. He put the volcano and the earthquakes and the boiling swamp and the hurricane out of his mind, and kept only one thing—absolute motion. The currents of blackness flowed past him, and then suddenly he was caught up by them and carried with them, and there was no time, no movement, no energy, no existence—nothing but the feeling of rest.

At the same time, lights began to flash on the instrument board. Yjul, in spite of his headache, began to throw levers. A mighty rumble of power shook the *Drifter* from stem to stem. She shivered and bucked against the sucking power of the mud, and Yjul threw still more quadrillions of ergs into the battle. Just to be sure they'd make it in time, the Bryd skipped into Yjul's mind and prodded him a little.

The ship reared and rocked. With jets spurting purple green flame for ten thousand miles, she roared up out of the swamp and surged into the sky above The Orphan at 1200 absolute metagalactic G's.

The Bryd took a deep breath. That had been close. It rolled into the warmest corner of Erle Bertron's mind and began to settle down. It was almost asleep when it remembered something. Having gone this far, it might as well go the whole way. Yawning and figuratively rubbing its eyes, it went out and looked around. The Scotch was all gone and all the bottles but one had gone down the disintichute.

The Bryd went back in time about one twenty-five-millionth of a millichron. It picked up the empty bottle so fast that even Fyllath couldn't have seen it. It set it up on the table, which now was steady, thank goodness, and filled it with Scotch whiskey.

It crawled back into Erle's mind and before it went to sleep it implanted the knowledge of the full bottle of scotch, and the last thing it remembered was Erle, his wrists unfastened, getting up from the chair and saying, "Let's have a drink to celebrate, dear," and Yjul, his headache gone, looking bright and refreshed, with Fyllath close at his side, and Ekno standing at the controls, happy because he was once more moving through space…

CHAPTER FOURTEEN

ON THE WAY home Ekno experimented with the new power and got the *Drifter* up to nearly 3200 metagalactic O's.

"That's not the limit," he said. "We have to stop and report to the general. The metagalaxy needs this new energy."

"Do you have any idea," Erle asked, "how fast it would go?"

"I wouldn't be surprised," Ekno told him, "if we could attain G's into the millions."

"The only trouble," Yjul pointed out, "is that you've got to have a lot of room to make a run like that—for it takes as long to slow down as it does to gather speed. If we were making the run to the Ninth Metagalaxy, with a million light years to work in, we'd probably find that we have suddenly multiplied the available energy in the Fourth Universe by infinity."

They passed the Sink and sent a neutrogram to the metagalactic listening post on Tarazed, advising Remiggon of the fate of Volmik and the success of the cosmodrive. Decelerating at an enormous rate, and using the waste power to feed back into the artificial gravity units in bow and stem which protected them from the lethal pressures set up by deceleration, they were met below Regulus by a carrier ship. It took them to Airlock 58, from which they had left a few days before—though it seemed like a lifetime.

Erle and Naomi and the three Century Plants went down the ramp and got on the brown lane to Remiggon's headquarters. The carrier ship was swarming with purple balls.

"Security precautions," said Yjul. "That ship with its engine is worth a fabulous sum. Agents from every metagalaxy in the universe will be looking for a way to get their hands on it. Remiggon is right in taking no chances."

A new secretary was in the general's office—a humanoid girl, a striking brunette with dark eyes and high cheekbones. Erle started to smile at her, but looked at Naomi and saw the storm gathering in her sea-green eyes, and changed his mind. The girl said, "His Excellency said you were to be admitted at once."

The general was waiting on his desk, under the black ceiling that showed the Milky Way, and when the door opened for them, the purple ball floated forward to meet them. For the first time the general displayed a little of the friendly exuberance Erle had always expected of him. However, he sobered quickly when Erle said, "The admiral and his wife were—one directly, the other indirectly—victims of Volmik, just before he died. We buried them in space."

There was a moment of hushed silence. Then, very quietly, the general began speaking, his voice tremulous with emotion. "He will be missed," he said, "by all of us. He was a man of great courage, with exceptional gifts of mind and heart. But we can rest assured that if he could have foreseen how soon he was to die—he would have made no other choice. This new source of energy is going to be a tremendous boon to the metagalaxy. There are many planets without moons, too far from their suns to receive heat, too old for tides, with no interior heat, no available fuel, no falling water, no radioactive cores. To them this energy will be an incalculable boon."

"One would think," said Erle, "that such a planet would not hold much attraction for sentient beings."

"Our planet," said Yjul, "has little to offer but desert, and yet we like it. We have learned to go out into the desert to stand for weeks at a time and gather strength."

"That is one of the astonishing things about the

metagalaxy. No matter what the conditions, a species doesn't like to leave it. We have a planet belonging to one of the double stars of Izar. Periodically it gets drawn between the two stars, and the temperature extremes would seem to make life impossible. There are no surroundings of interest, for the planet is nothing but flat sand.

"There is no water, no atmosphere, no wind, no change of any kind from century to century except the temperature—and yet a sentient race—a humanoid race—has evolved there, and likes the planet. The inhabitants are extremely vigorous, with unusual survival characteristics, as you can imagine. They may some day be valuable citizens of the metagalaxy."

"And by the way, you will be interested to know when the news of Volmik's death reached Alphirk, it precipitated a general uprising. All natural Alphirkians were hunted down and killed, and the androids now are operating the planet."

Naomi shuddered, "Worms? Why did they have to be so malicious?"

"It's hard to say. There is no reason why even a worm should not be an upright citizen, but I suppose their evolution let only the antisocial worms survive. However, they prepared their own doom, you might say, by building the androids."

The general finally rested on his desk. "There is now the problem of aligning more engines for us, Mr. Bertron. Do you think you are up to it? It will not be an easy task."

Erle nodded, "Undoubtedly it will be monotonous work, after what we've been through—but you own my contract."

"It's gratifying to have you agreeable. I think all of you should stay around the city until we are sure the conversion program is on its way."

"Whatever you say," said Yjul.

"You are feeling better, I hope."

Yjul's leaf-tips danced, "Never better in my life. When I

felt the power surge through that engine, I knew my troubles were over."

"The ladies, of course, will remain?"

"There is one formality," Erle said, "Naomi and I want to be married."

"Oh? Are you prepared to take an oath of loyalty and fidelity to Miss Castiliano?"

"I am."

"And you, Miss Castiliano?"

No sound came from Naomi. Erle turned to look at her. She was staring at him, her sea-green eyes inexpressibly soft. "You didn't tell me," she murmured.

Erle touched her arm, "His Excellency is waiting for an answer," he said.

She looked down at her brown legs, splendid in the chartreuse shorts. "I'm not dressed—and—you didn't warn me!"

"The question," Remiggon said, "is whether you do or do not want to marry this man."

She took her arm from around Erle's neck, "Your Excellency, I most certainly do."

"Then I pronounce you man and wife. Now about our plans for the coming—" He sighed and muttered to Yjul, "I doubt that either one of them is interested in plans on a metagalactic level."

ERLE WENT OUT in ships. He aligned engines as long as he could get the feeling of motion. The laboratory had already worked on a way of pairing an aligned engine with an unaligned one, so that in effect each engine could double itself indefinitely, but they were not having much success.

Erle didn't mind anyway. Their apartment was of glass bricks and silver trim, with the weather whatever they wanted to dial, doors that opened automatically—and never forgot to close themselves. There was an artificial moon and stars and even sunlight calibrated to Earth perspective, lights that turned on when one needed them, a stove that did its own shopping, and marketing and baked-perfect food of any description they might choose.

Or they could stroll through Regulus City in the evening, riding the autowalks, switching to crosswalks, transferring to the express lanes, watching the great metagalactic-liners unload their strange cargoes. They were on the 108th level, and they could ride the express escalators to the top and watch the blue fires raging over the dome. But mostly it was best to be in their apartment, together with each other but shut away from the nine billion inhabitants of the teeming city.

Often Naomi went on the alignment trips with him, to preserve, the general told them, their relative ages. There was so much travel beyond the speed of light that Naomi would soon find herself the older if they did not take precautions, the general said.

And there was the day when Erle found that he was going to be the father of the first Earth-baby born in Regulus City. There was quite a celebration. The general sent him a box of cigars and a case of Scotch and other presents.

They named the boy Benjam. A daughter came presently, and they called her Maryl. A second son came and was called Regulus. All this time Erle was aligning engines. It was interesting work, and the general insisted on making provisions for the children to take long trips at high accelerations. "Otherwise," he said, "you'd find your children older than yourselves."

Yjul and Fyllath and Ekno had long ago gone back to their home on a planet of Gamma Velorum.

Then one day the general called Erle into his office. "We have finally accomplished what we've worked on so long," he said. "The perfection of a machine to align new engines from those already aligned. Up to this time the metagalaxy was still in precarious circumstances. You have aligned a great many engines, but the total is small compared to our demands. However, now you may have a rest. You've never been sick and you've never asked for time off. You have accumulated a great deal of back pay also."

Erle shrugged. "Everything was furnished for our living. We haven't needed money."

"At any rate, our option on your services has ended. I have instructed my secretary to return your contract, with a voucher for all back pay, and tickets to Earth for your entire family."

But Erle stared. Suddenly he felt useless, unneeded. He stared at the general. "What am I going to do?"

The general chuckled. "You will never lack for useful work. Your long experience with the metagalactic government will be worth decillions of ergs—pardon me, millions of dollars, for in all the Fourth Universe there are few who are accepted to work for the metagalactic government. An honorable discharge from our service is worth almost any sum you can name—if you want it."

Erle stared at him. "What do you mean exactly?"

"You've been away from Earth quite a while. You may find conditions different there. Your usefulness to Earth may be different from what you imagine."

Erle said thoughtfully, "I wonder what Earth *is* like."

"Planets change, the same as towns. When you first go back, it's all strange to you. Then you stay a while and somebody else comes along, and the newcomer is always a stranger."

Erle drew smoke deep into his lungs. "There's one thing wrong. Naomi and I are normal and all of our children are normal. We won't fit in on Earth."

Remiggon seemed to take a deep breath. "I was sure you would think of that."

There was a step at his side, and Erle looked up to see Naomi. He got to his feet.

"Please, both sit down," said Remiggon. "I have a story to tell you."

They relaxed, and Remiggon seemed to rest for a moment, collecting his thoughts. "I want you always to remember that you have rendered a great service to the metagalaxy. There are twenty million ships flying the star lanes at high velocity. The old trajectory freighters are being towed in by tractor vessels and equipped with power units. No longer does a planet have to wait thousands of years to get an element it needs."

The girl came in with a sheet of zinc paper and gave it to Erle.

"That's your check for your work for us," said Remiggon.

Erle frowned. "It looks like a million and eighty thousand dollars. There must be some mistake."

Naomi caught her breath.

Remiggon went on, "One of our ships hit forty-eight thousand metagalactic G's on the run from Fomalhaut. A trip that used to be scheduled for every five hundred years now takes place every thirty days. It brings all the galaxies closer together—solves problems and creates problems."

"What kind does it create?" asked Erle.

"Administration, for one thing. Take real estate. Many beings have become trillionaires and quadrillionaires speculating on terminal planets. With space sold by the cubic foot, you can realize it's like old days on Earth to the third power—and a great deal more." Remiggon sighed. "However, we prefer those problems to the ones of war."

"I would think so," said Erle, still wondering about the check.

"We have kept track of affairs on Earth for you. I recall you loaned most of your advance to a four-legged man."

"Yes. He probably lost it on dice."

"No. He nursed it very carefully, and now—I'm happy to say— there's a B & W Midway on Jupiter that's worth a great deal more than that check. For the check is hardly more than a token—under the circumstances."

"I—" Erle could say no more.

"We protected your interests," said Remiggon. "Although I must say that Wollansbe himself did everything possible. However, the thing has gone through many hands since then."

"Wait a minute," said Naomi. "This check is for a *billion* and eighty *million* dollars!"

Remiggon nodded. "Quite right, Mrs. Bertron. You have brains as well as beauty."

Erle said, "Let me see that thing again."

She handed it to him.

"The answer is," said the general, "that you've been gone longer than you realize. The reversal effect of ultra-C speeds is real, and we've kept a careful log of your light-second time. That's why your wife and your children have been with you very often on your trips. The net result is that you and your wife are almost the same age as you were when you came here. Your children are in proportion. "You have no idea how long you've been gone, do you?"

"Not now," said Erle slowly, "I thought twelve or fifteen years."

"You're in for a shock," said Remiggon. "You left Earth just over nine hundred years ago."

Erle sat very still. Finally he looked at Naomi and saw her white face.

"You're both good, healthy specimens," said Remiggon, "and you will survive this next shock when I tell you that the race of *Homo sapiens* has been extinct for six hundred years."

Naomi gasped. Erle sat, dumbfounded. "Benjam is only fifteen years old," he said finally.

"Nine hund—" Naomi began, then said, "Then we are the only living representatives of human beings or Earth beings?"

"Almost. You certainly are the only living Earth entities who have ever seen Earth."

Erle said, "I'm sure you have more to tell us."

"As a matter of fact, I have." Remiggon seemed pleasantly amused. "The human race took a wrong turn in the evolutionary pattern. The metagalaxy cannot interfere with such things on a planetary level, but in this we had you two—both normal."

"But—"

"Earth is it beautiful planet," said Remiggon. "One of my favorites, with conditions perfect for propagation of a species."

"How could that be?" asked Naomi. "I don't want my children marrying one another."

"I anticipated that, and our scientists long ago went to the trouble of preserving—creating, you might almost say— another pair of Earth people."

"Created?" asked Naomi. "Then they aren't human!"

"Why not? They are derived from human genes."

"I don't think—" said Erle.

The purple ball floated into the air and stopped before them both, "There is another thing I forgot to tell you both. It has to do with your own genesis."

They both stared at him.

"As it happens, you never wondered why you both were normal, did you?"

"I assumed it just happened," said Erle, bracing himself.

"It could have—but it didn't."

Erle reached for Naomi's hand.

"You are both test-tube babies, you know."

Naomi looked white.

"It's nothing to be ashamed of," said Remiggon, "The scientists took human genes and chromosomes and eliminated all the neurotic ones. Even absolute motion and absolute pitch, as we found out later, were implanted by them as experiments."

Erle said slowly, "That might explain a lot of things."

Naomi said, "And that's how you got another pair of humans."

"It was almost too late," Remiggon admitted.

Naomi looked at Erle, "We have neither father nor mother," she said slowly.

"On the contrary," said the general, "the entire human race is your ancestor—as the entire human race to come, if there is any, will be your descendant."

"You mean," said Erle thoughtfully, "it is for us to say whether we want to continue the human race."

"That's about it."

Erle said slowly, "If we went back to Earth—no factories, no manufactured things at all would be available. We'd have to do it all by hand."

Naomi got out of the chair. He stood up, and she threw her arms around him. "I *would* like to go back home," she admitted.

That afternoon they were packing. The three children were excited. Erle looked up at Naomi and said, "Do you realize that Man did solve his own problems after all? The race didn't die out."

"But—"

"There was something in the genes of the scientists who made us," he said, "that impelled them. They didn't know why—but the qualities necessary to avoid extinction were present, and they used them. Man didn't end up in a cultural cul-de-sac after all."

But as he closed the trunk, a thought struck him. Remiggon, the old fraud! He had seen fit to have another couple made to go back to Earth with them. Had he put the suggestion and the ideas of procedure in the scientist's minds in the first place? Erle wouldn't have put it past him.

THE END

If you've enjoyed this book, you will not want to miss these terrific titles...

ARMCHAIR SCI-FI & HORROR DOUBLE NOVELS, $12.95 each

D-1   **THE GALAXY RAIDERS** by William P. McGivern
         SPACE STATION #1 by Frank Belknap Long

D-2   **THE PROGRAMMED PEOPLE** by Jack Sharkey
         SLAVES OF THE CRYSTAL BRAIN by William Carter Sawtelle

D-3   **YOU'RE ALL ALONE** by Fritz Leiber
         THE LIQUID MAN by Bernard C. Gilford

D-4   **CITADEL OF THE STAR LORDS** by Edmond Hamilton
         VOYAGE TO ETERNITY by Milton Lesser

D-5   **IRON MEN OF VENUS** by Don Wilcox
         THE MAN WITH ABSOLUTE MOTION by Noel Loomis

D-6   **WHO SOWS THE WIND...** by Rog Phillips
         THE PUZZLE PLANET by Robert A. W. Lowndes

D-7   **PLANET OF DREAD** by Murray Leinster
         TWICE UPON A TIME by Charles L. Fontenay

D-8   **THE TERROR OUT OF SPACE** by Dwight V. Swain
         QUEST OF THE GOLDEN APE by Ivar Jorgensen and Adam Chase

D-9   **SECRET OF MARRACOTT DEEP** by Henry Slesar
         PAWN OF THE BLACK FLEET by Mark Clifton.

D-10   **BEYOND THE RINGS OF SATURN** by Robert Moore Williams
         A MAN OBSESSED by Alan E. Nourse

ARMCHAIR SCIENCE FICTION CLASSICS, $12.95 each

C-1   **THE GREEN MAN**
         by Harold M. Sherman

C-2   **A TRACE OF MEMORY**
         By Keith Laumer

C-3   **INTO PLUTONIAN DEPTHS**
         by Stanton A. Coblentz

ARMCHAIR MASTERS OF SCIENCE FICTION SERIES, $16.95 each

M-1   **MASTERS OF SCIENCE FICTION, Vol. One**
         Bryce Walton—"Dark of the Moon" and other tales

M-2   **MASTERS OF SCIENCE FICTION, Vol. Two**
         Jerome Bixby—"One Way Street" and other tales

If you've enjoyed this book, you will not want to miss these terrific titles…

ARMCHAIR SCI-FI & HORROR DOUBLE NOVELS, $12.95 each

ARMCHAIR SCIENCE FICTION CLASSICS, $12.95 each

ARMCHAIR SCI-FI & HORROR GEMS SERIES, $12.95 each

If you've enjoyed this book, you will not want to miss these terrific titles…

ARMCHAIR SCI-FI & HORROR DOUBLE NOVELS, $12.95 each

D-21   **EMPIRE OF EVIL** by Robert Arnette
       THE SIGN OF THE TIGER by Alan E. Nourse & J. A. Meyer

D-22   **OPERATION SQUARE PEG** by Frank Belknap Long
       ENCHANTRESS OF VENUS by Leigh Brackett

D-23   **THE LIFE WATCH** by Lester del Rey
       CREATURES OF THE ABYSS by Murray Leinster

D-24   **LEGION OF LAZARUS** by Edmond Hamilton
       STAR HUNTER by Andre Norton

D-25   **EMPIRE OF WOMEN** by John Fletcher
       ONE OF OUR CITIES IS MISSING by Irving Cox

D-26   **THE WRONG SIDE OF PARADISE** by Raymond F. Jones
       THE INVOLUNTARY IMMORTALS by Rog Phillips

D-27   **EARTH QUARTER** by Damon Knight
       ENVOY TO NEW WORLDS by Keith Laumer

D-28   **SLAVES TO THE METAL HORDE** by Milton Lesser
       HUNTERS OUT OF TIME by Joseph E. Kelleam

D-29   **RX JUPITER SAVE US** by Ward Moore
       BEWARE THE USURPERS by Geoff St. Reynard

D-30   **SECRET OF THE SERPENT** by Don Wilcox
       CRUSADE ACROSS THE VOID by Dwight V. Swain

ARMCHAIR SCIENCE FICTION CLASSICS, $12.95 each

C-7   **THE SHAVER MYSTERY, Book One**
       by Richard S. Shaver

C-8   **THE SHAVER MYSTERY, Book Two**
       by Richard S. Shaver

C-9   **MURDER IN SPACE** by David V. Reed
       by David V. Reed

ARMCHAIR MASTERS OF SCIENCE FICTION SERIES, $16.95 each

M-3   **MASTERS OF SCIENCE FICTION, Vol. Three**
       Robert Sheckley, "The Perfect Woman" and other tales

M-4   **MASTERS OF SCIENCE FICTION, Vol. Four**
       Mack Reynolds, "Stowaway" and other tales